Edward Bulwer

The Coming Race

Edward Bulwer

The Coming Race

ISBN/EAN: 9783742823328

Manufactured in Europe, USA, Canada, Australia, Japa

Cover: Foto ©Andreas Hilbeck / pixelio.de

Manufactured and distributed by brebook publishing software
(www.brebook.com)

Edward Bulwer

The Coming Race

COLLECTION

OF

BRITISH AUTHORS

TAUCHNITZ EDITION.

VOL. 1318.

THE COMING RACE

BY

EDWARD BULWER, LORD LYTTON.

IN ONE VOLUME.

COLLECTION

OF

BRITISH AUTHORS

TAUCHNITZ EDITION.

VOL. 1318.

THE COMING RACE
BY EDWARD BULWER, LORD LYTTON.

. .

IN ONE VOLUME. . .

TAUCHNITZ EDITION.

By the same Author.

THE
COMING RACE

BY

EDWARD BULWER, LORD LYTTON.

COPYRIGHT EDITION.

LEIPZIG
BERNHARD TAUCHNITZ
1873.

INSCRIBED

TO

MAX MÜLLER

IN TRIBUTE

OF

RESPECT AND ADMIRATION.

THE COMING RACE.

—

CHAPTER I.

I am a native of——, in the United States of America. My ancestors migrated from England in the reign of Charles II.; and my grandfather was not undistinguished in the War of Independence. My family, therefore, enjoyed a somewhat high social position in right of birth; and being also opulent, they were considered disqualified for the public service. My father once ran for Congress, but was signally defeated by his tailor. After that event he interfered little in politics, and lived much in his library. I was the eldest of three sons, and sent at the age of sixteen to the old country, partly to complete my literary education, partly to commence my commercial training in a mercantile firm at Liverpool. My father died shortly after I was twenty-one; and being left well off, and having a

taste for travel and adventure, I resigned, for a
time, all pursuit of the almighty dollar, and became
a desultory wanderer over the face of the earth.

In the year 18—, happening to be in——, I
was invited by a professional engineer, with whom
I had made acquaintance, to visit the recesses of
the —— mine, upon which he was employed.

The reader will understand, ere he close this
narrative, my reason for concealing all clue to the
district of which I write, and will perhaps thank me
for refraining from any description that may tend
to its discovery.

Let me say, then, as briefly as possible, that I
accompanied the engineer into the interior of the
mine, and became so strangely fascinated by its
gloomy wonders, and so interested in my friend's
explorations, that I prolonged my stay in the neighbourhood, and descended daily, for some weeks,
into the vaults and galleries hollowed by nature
and art beneath the surface of the earth. The
engineer was persuaded that far richer deposits of
mineral wealth than had yet been detected, would
be found in a new shaft that had been commenced

under his operations. In piercing this shaft we came one day upon a chasm jagged and seemingly charred at the sides, as if burst asunder at some distant period by volcanic fires. Down this chasm my friend caused himself to be lowered in a 'cage,' having first tested the atmosphere by the safety-lamp. He remained nearly an hour in the abyss. When he returned he was very pale, and with an anxious, thoughtful expression of face, very different from its ordinary character, which was open, cheerful, and fearless.

He said briefly that the descent appeared to him unsafe, and leading to no result; and, suspending further operations in the shaft, we returned to the more familiar parts of the mine.

All the rest of that day the engineer seemed preoccupied by some absorbing thought. He was unusually taciturn, and there was a scared, bewildered look in his eyes, as that of a man who has seen a ghost. At night, as we two were sitting alone in the lodging we shared together near the mouth of the mine, I said to my friend,—

"Tell me frankly what you saw in that chasm:

I am sure it was something strange and terrible.
Whatever it be, it has left your mind in a state of
doubt. In such a case two heads are better than
one. Confide in me."

The engineer long endeavoured to evade my
inquiries; but as, while he spoke, he helped himself
unconsciously out of the brandy-flask to a degree
to which he was wholly unaccustomed, for he was
a very temperate man, his reserve gradually melted
away. He who would keep himself to himself
should imitate the dumb animals, and drink water.
At last he said, "I will tell you all. When the cage
stopped, I found myself on a ridge of rock; and
below me, the chasm, taking a slanting direction,
shot down to a considerable depth, the darkness of
which my lamp could not have penetrated. But
through it, to my infinite surprise, streamed upward
a steady brilliant light. Could it be any volcanic
fire? in that case, surely I should have felt the heat.
Still, if on this there was doubt, it was of the
utmost importance to our common safety to clear
it up. I examined the sides of the descent, and
found that I could venture to trust myself to the

irregular projections or ledges, at least for some
way. I left the cage and clambered down. As I
drew near and nearer to the light, the chasm became wider, and at last I saw, to my unspeakable
amaze, a broad level road at the bottom of the
abyss, illumined as far as the eye could reach by
what seemed artificial gas-lamps placed at regular
intervals, as in the thoroughfare of a great city;
and I heard confusedly at a distance a hum as of
human voices. I know, of course, that no rival
miners are at work in this district. Whose could
be those voices? What human hands could have
levelled that road and marshalled those lamps?

"The superstitious belief, common to miners,
that gnomes or fiends dwell within the bowels of
the earth, began to seize me. I shuddered at the
thought of descending further and braving the inhabitants of this nether valley. Nor indeed could
I have done so without ropes, as from the spot I
had reached to the bottom of the chasm the sides
of the rock sank down abrupt, smooth, and sheer.
I retraced my steps with some difficulty. Now I
have told you all."

"You will descend again?"

"I ought, yet I feel as if I durst not."

"A trusty companion halves the journey and doubles the courage. I will go with you. We will provide ourselves with ropes of suitable length and strength—and—pardon me—you must not drink more to-night. Our hands and feet must be steady and firm to-morrow."

———

CHAPTER II.

WITH the morning my friend's nerves were re-braced, and he was not less excited by curiosity than myself. Perhaps more; for he evidently believed in his own story, and I felt considerable doubt of it: not that he would have wilfully told an untruth, but that I thought he must have been under one of those hallucinations which seize on our fancy or our nerves in solitary, unaccustomed places, and in which we give shape to the formless and sound to the dumb.

We selected six veteran miners to watch our descent; and as the cage held only one at a time, the engineer descended first; and when he had gained the ledge at which he had before halted, the cage re-arose for me. I soon gained his side. We had provided ourselves with a strong coil of rope.

The light struck on my sight as it had done

the day before on my friend's. The hollow through
which it came sloped diagonally: it seemed to me
a diffused atmospheric light, not like that from fire,
but soft and silvery, as from a northern star.
Quitting the cage, we descended, one after the
other, easily enough, owing to the juts in the side,
till we reached the place at which my friend had
previously halted, and which was a projection just
spacious enough to allow us to stand abreast. From
this spot the chasm widened rapidly like the lower
end of a vast funnel, and I saw distinctly the valley,
the road, the lamps which my companion had
described. He had exaggerated nothing. I heard
the sounds he had heard—a mingled indescribable
hum as of voices and a dull tramp as of feet.
Straining my eye farther down, I clearly beheld at
a distance the outline of some large building. It
could not be mere natural rock, it was too symmetrical, with huge heavy Egyptian-like columns,
and the whole lighted as from within. I had about
me a small pocket-telescope, and by the aid of this
I could distinguish, near the building I mention,
two forms which seemed human, though I could not

be sure. At least they were living, for they moved, and both vanished within the building. We now proceeded to attach the end of the rope we had brought with us to the ledge on which we stood, by the aid of clamps and grappling-hooks, with which, as well as with necessary tools, we were provided.

We were almost silent in our work. We toiled like men afraid to speak to each other. One end of the rope being thus apparently made firm to the ledge, the other, to which we fastened a fragment of the rock, rested on the ground below, a distance of some fifty feet. I was a younger and a more active man than my companion, and having served on board ship in my boyhood, this mode of transit was more familiar to me than to him. In a whisper I claimed the precedence, so that when I gained the ground I might serve to hold the rope more steady for his descent. I got safely to the ground beneath, and the engineer now began to lower himself. But he had scarcely accomplished ten feet of the descent, when the fastenings, which we had fancied so secure, gave way, or rather the rock it-

self proved treacherous and crumbled beneath the
strain; and the unhappy man was precipitated to
the bottom, falling just at my feet, and bringing
down with his fall splinters of the rock, one of
which, fortunately but a small one, struck and for
the time stunned me. When I recovered my senses
I saw my companion an inanimate mass beside me,
life utterly extinct. While I was bending over his
corpse in grief and horror, I heard close at hand a
strange sound between a snort and a hiss; and
turning instinctively to the quarter from which it
came, I saw emerging from a dark fissure in the
rock a vast and terrible head, with open jaws and
dull, ghastly, hungry eyes—the head of a monstrous
reptile resembling that of the crocodile or alligator,
but infinitely larger than the largest creature of that
kind I had ever beheld in my travels. I started to
my feet and fled down the valley at my utmost
speed. I stopped at last, ashamed of my panic and
my flight, and returned to the spot on which I had
left the body of my friend. It was gone; doubtless
the monster had already drawn it into its den and
devoured it. The rope and the grappling-hooks

still lay where they had fallen, but they afforded me no chance of return: it was impossible to re-attach them to the rock above, and the sides of the rock were too sheer and smooth for human steps to clamber. I was alone in this strange world, amidst the bowels of the earth.

———

CHAPTER III.

SLOWLY and cautiously I went my solitary way down the lamplit road and towards the large building I have described. The road itself seemed like a great Alpine pass, skirting rocky mountains of which the one through whose chasms I had descended formed a link. Deep below to the left lay a vast valley, which presented to my astonished eye the unmistakable evidences of art and culture. There were fields covered with a strange vegetation, similar to none I have seen above the earth; the colour of it not green, but rather of a dull leaden hue or of a golden red.

There were lakes and rivulets which seemed to have been curbed into artificial banks; some of pure water, others that shone like pools of naphtha. At my right hand, ravines and defiles opened amidst the rocks, with passes between, evidently constructed by art, and bordered by trees resembling,

for the most part, gigantic ferns, with exquisite
varieties of feathery foliage, and stems like those of
the palm-tree. Others were more like the cane-
plant, but taller, bearing large clusters of flowers.
Others, again, had the form of enormous fungi, with
short thick stems supporting a wide dome-like roof,
from which either rose or drooped long slender
branches. The whole scene behind, before, and
beside me, far as the eye could reach, was brilliant
with innumerable lamps. The world without a sun
was bright and warm as an Italian landscape at
noon, but the air less oppressive, the heat softer.
Nor was the scene before me void of signs of habitation. I could distinguish at a distance, whether
on the banks of lake or rivulet, or half-way upon
eminences, embedded amidst the vegetation, buildings that must surely be the homes of men. I could
even discover, though far off, forms that appeared
to me human moving amidst the landscape. As I
paused to gaze, I saw to the right, gliding quickly
through the air, what appeared a small boat, impelled by sails shaped like wings. It soon passed
out of sight, descending amidst the shades of a

2*

forest. Right above me there was no sky, but only
a cavernous roof. This roof grew higher and higher
at the distance of the landscapes beyond, till it became imperceptible, as an atmosphere of haze
formed itself beneath.

Continuing my walk, I started,—from a bush
that resembled a great tangle of sea-weeds, interspersed with fern-like shrubs and plants of large
leafage shaped like that of the aloe or prickly pear,
—a curious animal about the size and shape of a
deer. But as, after bounding away a few paces, it
turned round and gazed at me inquisitively, I perceived that it was not like any species of deer now
extant above the earth, but it brought instantly to
my recollection a plaster cast I had seen in some
museum of a variety of the elk stag, said to have
existed before the Deluge. The creature seemed
tame enough, and, after inspecting me a moment
or two, began to graze on the singular herbage
around undismayed and careless.

CHAPTER IV.

I NOW came in full sight of the building. Yes,
it had been made by hands, and hollowed partly
out of a great rock. I should have supposed it at
the first glance to have been of the earliest form of
Egyptian architecture. It was fronted by huge
columns, tapering upward from massive plinths, and
with capitals that, as I came nearer, I perceived to
be more ornamental and more fantastically graceful
than Egyptian architecture allows. As the Corin-
thian capital mimics the leaf of the acanthus, so the
capitals of these columns imitated the foliage of the
vegetation neighbouring them, some aloe-like, some
fern-like. And now there came out of this building
a form—human;—was it human! It stood on the
broad way and looked around, beheld me and approached. It came within a few yards of me, and
at the sight and presence of it an indescribable awe
and tremor seized me, rooting my feet to the ground.

It reminded me of symbolical images of Genius or
Demon that are seen on Etruscan vases or limned
on the walls of Eastern sepulchres—images that
borrow the outlines of man, and are yet of another
race. It was tall, not gigantic, but tall as the tallest
men below the height of giants.

Its chief covering seemed to me to be composed
of large wings folded over its breast and reaching
to its knees; the rest of its attire was composed of
an under tunic and leggings of some thin fibrous
material. It wore on its head a kind of tiara that
shone with jewels, and carried in its right hand a
slender staff of bright metal like polished steel.
But the face! it was that which inspired my awe
and my terror. It was the face of man, but yet of
a type of man distinct from our known extant races.
The nearest approach to it in outline and expression is the face of the sculptured sphinx—so regular
in its calm, intellectual, mysterious beauty. Its
colour was peculiar, more like that of the red man
than any other variety of our species, and yet different from it—a richer and a softer hue, with large
black eyes, deep and brilliant, and brows arched as

a semicircle. The face was beardless; but a nameless something in the aspect, tranquil though the expression, and beauteous though the features, roused that instinct of danger which the sight of a tiger or serpent arouses. I felt that this manlike image was endowed with forces inimical to man. As it drew near, a cold shudder came over me. I fell on my knees and covered my face with my hands.

———

CHAPTER V.

A voice accosted me—a very quiet and very musical key of voice—in a language of which I could not understand a word, but it served to dispel my fear. I uncovered my face and looked up. The stranger (I could scarcely bring myself to call him man) surveyed me with an eye that seemed to read to the very depths of my heart. He then placed his left hand on my forehead, and with the staff in his right gently touched my shoulder. The effect of this double contact was magical. In place of my former terror there passed into me a sense of contentment, of joy, of confidence in myself and in the being before me. I rose and spoke in my own language. He listened to me with apparent attention, but with a slight surprise in his looks; and shook his head, as if to signify that I was not understood. He then took me by the hand and led me in silence to the building. The entrance was

open—indeed there was no door to it. We entered
an immense hall, lighted by the same kind of lustre
as in the scene without, but diffusing a fragrant
odour. The floor was in large tesselated blocks of
precious metals, and partly covered with a sort of
matlike carpeting. A strain of low music, above
and around, undulated as if from invisible instruments, seeming to belong naturally to the place,
just as the sound of murmuring waters belongs to
a rocky landscape, or the warble of birds to vernal
groves.

A figure, in a simpler garb than that of my
guide, but of similar fashion, was standing motionless near the threshold. My guide touched it twice
with his staff, and it put itself into a rapid and gliding movement, skimming noiselessly over the floor.
Gazing on it, I then saw that it was no living form,
but a mechanical automaton. It might be two minutes after it vanished through a doorless opening,
half screened by curtains at the other end of the
hall, when through the same opening advanced a
boy of about twelve years old, with features closely
resembling those of my guide, so that they seemed

to me evidently son and father. On seeing me the
child uttered a cry, and lifted a staff like that borne
by my guide, as if in menace. At a word from the
elder he dropped it. The two then conversed for
some moments, examining me while they spoke.
The child touched my garments, and stroked my
face with evident curiosity, uttering a sound like a
laugh, but with an hilarity more subdued than the
mirth of our laughter. Presently the roof of the hall
opened, and a platform descended, seemingly constructed on the same principle as the "lifts" used in
hotels and warehouses for mounting from one story
to another.

The stranger placed himself and the child on
the platform, and motioned to me to do the same,
which I did. We ascended quickly and safely, and
alighted in the midst of a corridor with doorways
on either side.

Through one of these doorways I was conducted
into a chamber fitted up with an Oriental splendour;
the walls were tessalated with spars, and metals,
and uncut jewels; cushions and divans abounded;
apertures as for windows, but unglazed, were made

in the chamber, opening to the floor; and as I
passed along I observed that these openings led
into spacious balconies, and commanded views of
the illumined landscape without. In cages suspended
from the ceiling there were birds of strange form
and bright plumage, which at our entrance set up
a chorus of song, modulated into tune as is that of
our piping bullfinches. A delicious fragrance, from
censers of gold elaborately sculptured, filled the air.
Several automata, like the one I had seen, stood
dumb and motionless by the walls. The stranger
placed me beside him on a divan, and again
spoke to me, and again I spoke, but without the
least advance towards understanding each other.

But now I began to feel the effects of the blow
I had received from the splinters of the falling rock
more acutely than I had done at first.

There came over me a sense of sickly faintness,
accompanied with acute, lancinating pains in the
head and neck. I sank back on the seat, and strove
in vain to stifle a groan. On this the child, who
had hitherto seemed to eye me with distrust or dis-

like, knelt by my side to support me; taking one of
my hands in both his own, he approached his lips
to my forehead, breathing on it softly. In a few
moments my pain ceased; a drowsy, happy calm
crept over me; I fell asleep.

How long I remained in this state I know not,
but when I woke I felt perfectly restored. My eyes
opened upon a group of silent forms, seated around
me in the gravity and quietude of Orientals—all
more or less like the first stranger; the same man-
tling wings, the same fashion of garment, the same
sphinx-like faces, with the deep dark eyes and red
man's colour; above all, the same type of race—
race akin to man's, but infinitely stronger of form
and grander of aspect, and inspiring the same un-
utterable feeling of dread. Yet each countenance
was mild and tranquil, and even kindly in its expression. And, strangely enough, it seemed to me
that in this very calm and benignity consisted the
secret of the dread which the countenances inspired.
They seemed as void of the lines and shadows
which care and sorrow, and passion and sin, leave
upon the faces of men, as are the faces of sculp-

tured gods, or as, in the eyes of Christian mourners, seem the peaceful brows of the dead.

I felt a warm hand on my shoulder; it was the child's. In his eyes there was a sort of lofty pity and tenderness, such as that with which we may gaze on some suffering bird or butterfly. I shrank from that touch—I shrank from that eye. I was vaguely impressed with a belief that, had he so pleased, that child could have killed me as easily as a man can kill a bird or a butterfly. The child seemed pained at my repugnance, quitted me, and placed himself beside one of the windows. The others continued to converse with each other in a low tone, and by their glances towards me I could perceive that I was the object of their conversation. One in especial seemed to be urging some proposal affecting me on the being whom I had first met, and this last by his gesture seemed about to assent to it, when the child suddenly quitted his post by the window, placed himself between me and the other forms, as if in protection, and spoke quickly and eagerly. By some intuition or instinct I felt that the child I had before so dreaded was plead-

ing in my behalf. Ere he had ceased another
stranger entered the room. He appeared older than
the rest, though not old; his countenance, less
smoothly serene than theirs, though equally regular
in its features, seemed to me to have more the
touch of a humanity akin to my own. He listened
quietly to the words addressed to him, first by my
guide, next by two others of the group, and lastly
by the child; then turned towards myself, and addressed me, not by words, but by signs and gestures.
These I fancied that I perfectly understood, and I
was not mistaken. I comprehended that he inquired
whence I came. I extended my arm and pointed
towards the road which had led me from the chasm
in the rock; then an idea seized me. I drew forth
my pocket-book and sketched on one of its blank
leaves a rough design of the ledge of the rock, the
rope, myself clinging to it; then of the cavernous
rock below, the head of the reptile, the lifeless form
of my friend. I gave this primitive kind of hiero-
glyph to my interrogator, who, after inspecting it
gravely, handed it to his next neighbour, and it thus
passed round the group. The being I had at first

encountered then said a few words, and the child,
who approached and looked at my drawing, nodded
as if he comprehended its purport, and, returning
to the window, expanded the wings attached to his
form, shook them once or twice, and then launched
himself into space without. I started up in amaze
and hastened to the window. The child was already
in the air, buoyed on his wings, which he did not
flap to and fro as a bird does, but which were
elevated over his head, and seemed to bear him
steadily aloft without effort of his own. His flight
seemed as swift as any eagle's; and I observed that
it was towards the rock whence I had descended,
of which the outline loomed visible in the brilliant
atmosphere. In a very few minutes he returned,
skimming through the opening from which he had
gone, and dropping on the floor the rope and
grappling-hooks I had left at the descent from the
chasm. Some words in a low tone passed between
the beings present: one of the group touched an
automaton, which started forward and glided from
the room; then the last comer, who had addressed
me by gestures, rose, took me by the hand, and led

me into the corridor. There the platform by which
I had mounted awaited us; we placed ourselves on
it and were lowered into the hall below. My new
companion, still holding me by the hand, conducted
me from the building into a street (so to speak)
that stretched beyond it, with buildings on either
side, separated from each other by gardens bright
with rich-coloured vegetation and strange flowers.
Interspersed amidst these gardens, which were
divided from each other by low walls, or walking
slowly along the road, were many forms similar to
those I had already seen. Some of the passers-by,
on observing me, approached my guide, evidently
by their tones, looks, and gestures addressing to
him inquiries about myself. In a few moments a
crowd collected round us, examining me with great
interest, as if I were some rare wild animal. Yet
even in gratifying their curiosity they preserved a
grave and courteous demeanour; and after a few
words from my guide, who seemed to me to depre-
cate obstruction in our road, they fell back with a
stately inclination of head, and resumed their own
way with tranquil indifference. Midway in this

thoroughfare we stopped at a building that differed
from those we had hitherto passed, inasmuch as it
formed three sides of a vast court, at the angles of
which were lofty pyramidal towers; in the open
space between the sides was a circular fountain of
colossal dimensions, and throwing up a dazzling
spray of what seemed to me fire. We entered the
building through an open doorway and came into
an enormous hall, in which were several groups of
children, all apparently employed in work as at
some great factory. There was a huge engine in
the wall which was in full play, with wheels and
cylinders, and resembling our own steam-engines,
except that it was richly ornamented with precious
stones and metals, and appeared to emit a pale
phosphorescent atmosphere of shifting light. Many
of the children were at some mysterious work on
this machinery, others were seated before tables. I
was not allowed to linger long enough to examine
into the nature of their employment. Not one young
voice was heard—not one young face turned to
gaze on us. They were all still and indifferent as

may be ghosts, through the midst of which pass un-
noticed the forms of the living.

Quitting this hall, my guide led me through a
gallery richly painted in compartments, with a bar-
baric mixture of gold in the colours, like pictures
by Louis Cranach. The subjects described on these
walls appeared to my glance as intended to illustrate
events in the history of the race amidst which I was
admitted. In all there were figures, most of them
like the manlike creatures I had seen, but not all
in the same fashion of garb, nor all with wings;
There were also the effigies of various animals and
birds wholly strange to me, with backgrounds
depicting landscapes or buildings. So far as my
imperfect knowledge of the pictorial art would allow
me to form an opinion, these paintings seemed very
accurate in design and very rich in colouring, showing a perfect knowledge of perspective, but their
details not arranged according to the rules of composition acknowledged by our artists—wanting, as
it were, a centre; so that the effect was vague, scattered, confused, bewildering—they were like hetero-
geneous fragments of a dream of art.

We now came into a room of moderate size, in
which was assembled what I afterwards knew to be
the family of my guide, seated at a table spread as
for repast. The forms thus grouped were those of
my guide's wife, his daughter, and two sons. I recognised at once the difference between the two
sexes, though the two females were of taller stature
and ampler proportions than the males; and their
countenances, if still more symmetrical in outline
and contour, were devoid of the softness and timidity
of expression which give charm to the face of woman as seen on the earth above. The wife wore
no wings, the daughter wore wings longer than those
of the males.

My guide uttered a few words, on which all the
persons seated rose, and with that peculiar mildness
of look and manner which I have before noticed,
and which is, in truth, the common attribute of this
formidable race, they saluted me according to their
fashion, which consists in laying the right hand very
gently on the head and uttering a soft sibilant
monosyllable—S.Si, equivalent to "Welcome."

The mistress of the house then seated me beside

her, and heaped a golden platter before me from one of the dishes.

While I ate (and though the viands were new to me, I marvelled more at the delicacy than the strangeness of their flavour), my companions conversed quietly, and, so far as I could detect, with polite avoidance of any direct reference to myself, or any obtrusive scrutiny of my appearance. Yet I was the first creature of that variety of the human race to which I belong that they had ever beheld, and was consequently regarded by them as a most curious and abnormal phenomenon. But all rudeness is unknown to this people, and the youngest child is taught to despise any vehement emotional demonstration. When the meal was ended, my guide again took me by the hand, and, re-entering the gallery, touched a metallic plate inscribed with strange figures, and which I rightly conjectured to be of the nature of our telegraphs. A platform descended, but this time we mounted to a much greater height than in the former building, and found ourselves in a room of moderate dimensions, and which in its general character had much that might be familiar to the associations of a visitor from the upper world. There were shelves on the wall containing what appeared to be books, and indeed were so; mostly very small, like our diamond duodecimos, shaped in the fashion of our volumes, and bound in fine sheets of metal. There were several curious-looking pieces of mechanism scattered about, apparently models, such as might be seen in the study of any professional mechanician. For automata (mechanical contrivances which, with these people, answer the ordinary purposes of domestic service) stood phantomlike at each angle in the wall. In a recess was a low couch, or bed with pillows. A window, with curtains of some fibrous material drawn aside, opened upon a large balcony. My host stepped out into the balcony; I followed him. We were on the uppermost story of one of the angular pyramids; the view beyond was of a wild and solemn beauty impossible to describe, —the vast ranges of precipitous rock which formed the distant background, the intermediate valleys of mystic many-coloured herbage, the flash of waters, many of them like streams of roseate flame, the

serene lustre diffused over all by myriads of lamps,
combined to form a whole of which no words of
mine can convey adequate description; so splendid
was it, yet so sombre; so lovely, yet so awful.

But my attention was soon diverted from these
nether landscapes. Suddenly there arose, as from
the streets below, a burst of joyous music; then a
winged form soared into the space; another, as in
chase of the first, another and another; others after
others, till the crowd grew thick and the number
countless. But how describe the fantastic grace of
these forms in their undulating movements! They
appeared engaged in some sport or amusement;
now forming into opposite squadrons; now scatter-
ing; now each group threading the other, soaring,
descending, interweaving, severing; all in measured
time to the music below, as if in the dance of the
fabled Peri.

I turned my gaze on my host in a feverish
wonder. I ventured to place my hand on the large
wings that lay folded on his breast, and in doing
so a slight shock as of electricity passed through
me. I recoiled in fear; my host smiled, and, as if

courteously to gratify my curiosity, slowly expanded his pinions. I observed that his garment beneath then became dilated as a bladder that fills with air. The arms seemed to slide into the wings, and in another moment he had launched himself into the luminous atmosphere, and hovered there, still, and with outspread wings, as an eagle that basks in the sun. Then, rapidly as an eagle swoops, he rushed downwards into the midst of one of the groups, skimming through the midst, and as suddenly again soaring aloft. Thereon, three forms, in one of which I thought to recognise my host's daughter, detached themselves from the rest, and followed him as a bird sportively follows a bird. My eyes, dazzled with the lights and bewildered by the throngs, ceased to distinguish the gyrations and evolutions of these winged playmates, till presently my host re-emerged from the crowd and alighted at my side.

The strangeness of all I had seen began now to operate fast on my senses; my mind itself began to wander. Though not inclined to be superstitious, nor hitherto believing that man could be brought

into bodily communication with demons, I felt the
terror and the wild excitement with which, in the
Gothic ages, a traveller might have persuaded himself that he witnessed a *sabbat* of fiends and witches.
I have a vague recollection of having attempted
with vehement gesticulation, and forms of exorcism,
and loud incoherent words, to repel my courteous
and indulgent host; of his mild endeavours to calm
and soothe me; of his intelligent conjecture that my
fright and bewilderment were occasioned by the
difference of form and movement between us which
the wings that had excited my marvelling curiosity
had, in exercise, made still more strongly perceptible;
of the gentle smile with which he had sought to
dispel my alarm by dropping the wings to the
ground and endeavouring to show me that they
were but a mechanical contrivance. That sudden
transformation did but increase my horror, and as
extreme fright often shows itself by extreme daring,
I sprang at his throat like a wild beast. On an instant I was felled to the ground as by an electric
shock, and the last confused images floating before
my sight ere I became wholly insensible, were the

form of my host kneeling beside me with one hand on my forehead, and the beautiful calm face of his daughter, with large, deep, inscrutable eyes intently fixed upon my own.

————

CHAPTER VI

I REMAINED in this unconscious state, as I afterwards learned, for many days, even for some weeks, according to our computation of time. When I recovered I was in a strange room, my host and all his family were gathered round me, and to my utter amaze my host's daughter accosted me in my own language with but a slightly foreign accent.

"How do you feel?" she asked.

It was some moments before I could overcome my surprise enough to falter out, "You know my language! How! Who and what are you?"

My host smiled and motioned to one of his sons, who then took from a table a number of thin metallic sheets on which were traced drawings of various figures—a house, a tree, a bird, a man, &c.

In these designs I recognised my own style of drawing. Under each figure was written the name of it in my language, and in my writing; and in another handwriting a word strange to me beneath it.

Said the host, "Thus we began; and my daughter Zee, who belongs to the College of Sages, has been your instructress and ours too."

Zee then placed before me other metallic sheets, on which, in my writing, words first, and then sentences, were inscribed. Under each word and each sentence strange characters in another hand. Rallying my senses, I comprehended that thus a rude dictionary had been effected. Had it been done while I was dreaming? "That is enough now," said Zee, in a tone of command. "Repose and take food."

CHAPTER VII.

A ROOM to myself was assigned to me in this
vast edifice. It was prettily and fantastically arranged, but without any of the splendour of metal-
work or gems which was displayed in the more
public apartments. The walls were hung with a
variegated matting made from the stalks and fibres
of plants, and the floor carpeted with the same.

The bed was without curtains, its supports of
iron resting on balls of crystal; the coverings, of a
thin white substance resembling cotton. There
were sundry shelves containing books. A curtained
recess communicated with an aviary filled with singing-birds, of which I did not recognise one resembling those I have seen on earth, except a
beautiful species of dove, though this was distinguished from our doves by a tall crest of bluish
plumes. All these birds had been trained to sing
in artful tunes, and greatly exceeded the skill of

our piping bullfinches, which can rarely achieve
more than two tunes, and cannot, I believe, sing
those in concert. One might have supposed one's
self at an opera in listening to the voices in my
aviary. There were duets and trios, and quartettes
and choruses, all arranged as in one piece of music.
Did I want to silence the birds? I had but to draw
a curtain over the aviary, and their song hushed as
they found themselves left in the dark. Another
opening formed a window, not glazed, but on
touching a spring, a shutter ascended from the
floor, formed of some substance less transparent
than glass, but still sufficiently pellucid to allow a
softened view of the scene without. To this window
was attached a balcony, or rather hanging-garden,
wherein grew many graceful plants and brilliant
flowers. The apartment and its appurtenances had
thus a character, if strange in detail, still familiar,
as a whole, to modern notions of luxury, and
would have excited admiration if found attached to
the apartments of an English duchess or a fashion-
able French author. Before I arrived this was Zee's
chamber; she had hospitably assigned it to me.

Some hours after the waking up which is described in my last chapter, I was lying alone on my couch trying to fix my thoughts on conjecture as to the nature and genus of the people amongst whom I was thrown, when my host and his daughter Zee entered the room. My host, still speaking my native language, inquired, with much politeness, whether it would be agreeable to me to converse, or if I preferred solitude. I replied, that I should feel much honoured and obliged by the opportunity offered me to express my gratitude for the hospitality and civilities I had received in a country to which I was a stranger, and to learn enough of its customs and manners not to offend through ignorance.

As I spoke, I had of course risen from my couch; but Zee, much to my confusion, curtly ordered me to lie down again, and there was something in her voice and eye, gentle as both were, that compelled my obedience. She then seated herself unconcernedly at the foot of my bed, while her father took his place on a divan a few feet distant.

"But what part of the world do you come from,"

asked my host, "that we should appear so strange
to you, and you to us? I have seen individual
specimens of nearly all the races differing from our
own, except the primeval savages who dwell in the
most desolate and remote recesses of uncultivated
nature, unacquainted with other light than that they
obtain from volcanic fires, and contented to grope
their way in the dark, as do many creeping, crawling,
and even flying things. But certainly you cannot
be a member of those barbarous tribes, nor, on the
other hand, do you seem to belong to any civilised
people."

I was somewhat nettled at this last observation,
and replied that I had the honour to belong to one
of the most civilised nations of the earth; and that,
so far as light was concerned, while I admired the
ingenuity and disregard of expense with which my
host and his fellow-citizens had contrived to illumine
the regions unpenetrated by the rays of the sun, yet
I could not conceive how any who had once beheld
the orbs of heaven could compare to their lustre the
artificial lights invented by the necessities of man.
But my host said he had seen specimens of most of

the races differing from his own, save the wretched barbarians he had mentioned. Now, was it possible that he had never been on the surface of the earth, or could he only be referring to communities buried within its entrails?

My host was for some moments silent; his countenance showed a degree of surprise which the people of that race very rarely manifest under any circumstances, howsoever extraordinary. But Zee was more intelligent, and exclaimed, "So you see, my father, that there is truth in the old tradition; there always is truth in every tradition commonly believed in all times and by all tribes."

"Zee," said my host, mildly, "you belong to the College of Sages, and ought to be wiser than I am; but, as chief of the Light-preserving Council, it is my duty to take nothing for granted till it is proved to the evidence of my own senses." Then, turning to me, he asked me several questions about the surface of the earth and the heavenly bodies; upon which, though I answered him to the best of my knowledge, my answers seemed not to satisfy nor convince him. He shook his head quietly, and,

changing the subject rather abruptly, asked how I
had come down from what he was pleased to call
one world to the other. I answered, that under the
surface of the earth there were mines containing
minerals, or metals, essential to our wants and our
progress in all arts and industries; and I then briefly
explained the manner in which, while exploring one
of these mines, I and my ill-fated friend had ob-
tained a glimpse of the regions into which we had
descended, and how the descent had cost him his
life; appealing to the rope and grappling-hooks that
the child had brought to the house in which I had
been at first received, as a witness of the truthfulness of my story.

My host then proceeded to question me as to
the habits and modes of life among the races on
the upper earth, more especially among those considered to be the most advanced in that civilisation
which he was pleased to define "the art of diffusing
throughout a community the tranquil happiness
which belongs to a virtuous and well-ordered household." Naturally desiring to represent in the most
favourable colours the world from which I came, I

touched but slightly, though indulgently, on the antiquated and decaying institutions of Europe, in
order to expatiate on the present grandeur and pro-
spective pre-eminence of that glorious American
Republic, in which Europe enviously seeks its model
and tremblingly foresees its doom. Selecting for an
example of the social life of the United States that
city in which progress advances at the fastest rate,
I indulged in an animated description of the moral
habits of New York. Mortified to see, by the faces
of my listeners, that I did not make the favourable
impression I had anticipated, I elevated my theme;
dwelling on the excellence of democratic institutions,
their promotion of tranquil happiness by the government of party, and the mode in which they diffused
such happiness throughout the community by pre-
ferring, for the exercise of power and the acquisi-
tion of honours, the lowliest citizens in point of
property, education, and character. Fortunately re-
collecting the peroration of a speech, on the purify-
ing influences of American democracy and their
destined spread over the world, made by a certain
eloquent senator (for whose vote in the Senate a

Railway Company, to which my two brothers belonged, had just paid 20,000 dollars), I wound up by repeating its glowing predictions of the magnificent future that smiled upon mankind—when the flag of freedom should float over an entire continent, and two hundred millions of intelligent citizens, accustomed from infancy to the daily use of revolvers, should apply to a cowering universe the doctrine of the Patriot Monroe.

When I had concluded, my host gently shook his head, and fell into a musing study, making a sign to me and his daughter to remain silent while he reflected. And after a time he said, in a very earnest and solemn tone, "If you think, as you say, that you, though a stranger, have received kindness at the hands of me and mine, I adjure you to reveal nothing to any other of our people respecting the world from which you came, unless, on consideration, I give you permission to do so. Do you consent to this request?"

"Of course I pledge my word to it," said I, somewhat amazed; and I extended my right hand to grasp his. But he placed my hand gently on his

4*

forehead and his own right hand on my breast,
which is the custom among this race in all matters
of promise or verbal obligations.   Then turning to
his daughter, he said, "And you, Zee, will not repeat
to any one what the stranger has said, or may say,
to me or to you, of a world other than our own."
Zee rose and kissed her father on the temples, saying, with a smile, "A Gy's tongue is wanton, but
love can fetter it fast. And if, my father, you fear
lest a chance word from me or yourself could expose our community to danger, by a desire to ex-
plore a world beyond us, will not a wave of the
vril, properly impelled, wash even the memory of
what we have heard the stranger say out of the
tablets of the brain?"

"What is vril?" I asked.

Therewith Zee began to enter into an explana-
tion of which I understood very little, for there is
no word in any language I know which is an exact
synonym for vril. I should call it electricity, except
that it comprehends in its manifold branches other
forces of nature, to which, in our scientific nomen-
clature, differing names are assigned, such as mag-

netism, galvanism, &c. These people consider that in
vril they have arrived at the unity in natural energic
agencies, which has been conjectured by many philosophers above ground, and which Faraday thus
intimates under the more cautious term of correla-
tion:—

"I have long held an opinion," says that illustrious experimentalist, "almost amounting to a conviction, in common, I believe, with many other
lovers of natural knowledge, that the various forms
under which the forces of matter are made manifest
have one common origin; or, in other words, are
so directly related and mutually dependent, that
they are convertible, as it were, into one another,
and possess equivalents of power in their action."

These subterranean philosophers assert that by
one operation of vril, which Faraday would perhaps
call 'atmospheric magnetism,' they can influence the
variations of temperature—in plain words, the
weather; that by other operations, akin to those ascribed to mesmerism, electro-biology, odic force, &c.,
but applied scientifically through vril conductors,
they can exercise influence over minds, and bodies

animal and vegetable, to an extent not surpassed in
the romances of our mystics. To all such agencies
they give the common name of vril. Zee asked me
if, in my world, it was not known that all the faculties
of the mind could be quickened to a degree unknown in the waking state, by trance or vision, in
which the thoughts of one brain could be transmitted to another, and knowledge be thus rapidly
interchanged.   I replied, that there were among us
stories told of such trance or vision, and that I had
heard much and seen something of the mode in
which they were artificially effected, as in mesmeric
clairvoyance; but that these practices had fallen much
into disuse or contempt, partly because of the gross
impostures to which they had been made sub-
servient, and partly because, even where the effects
upon certain abnormal constitutions were genuinely
produced, the effects, when fairly examined and
analysed, were very unsatisfactory—not to be relied
upon for any systematic truthfulness or any practical
purpose, and rendered very mischievous to credulous
persons by the superstitions they tended to produce.
Zee received my answers with much benignant atten-

tion, and said that similar instances of abuse and
credulity had been familiar to their own scientific
experience in the infancy of their knowledge, and
while the properties of vril were misapprehended,
but that she reserved further discussion on this subject till I was more fitted to enter into it. She contented herself with adding, that it was through the
agency of vril, while I had been placed in the state
of trance, that I had been made acquainted with
the rudiments of their language; and that she and
her father, who, alone of the family, took the pains
to watch the experiment, had acquired a greater
proportionate knowledge of my language than I of
their own; partly because my language was much
simpler than theirs, comprising far less of complex
ideas; and partly because their organisation was, by
hereditary culture, much more ductile and more
readily capable of acquiring knowledge than mine.
At this I secretly demurred; and having had, in the
course of a practical life, to sharpen my wits, whether
at home or in travel, I could not allow that my
cerebral organisation could possibly be duller than
that of people who had lived all their lives by lamp-

light. However, while I was thus thinking, Zee
quietly pointed her forefinger at my forehead and
sent me to sleep.

————

CHAPTER VIII

WHEN I once more awoke I saw by my bedside the child who had brought the rope and grappling-hooks to the house in which I had been first received, and which, as I afterwards learned, was the residence of the chief magistrate of the tribe. The child, whose name was Taë (pronounced Tar-ee), was the magistrate's eldest son. I found that during my last sleep or trance I had made still greater advance in the language of the country, and could converse with comparative ease and fluency.

This child was singularly handsome, even for the beautiful race to which he belonged, with a countenance very manly in aspect for his years, and with a more vivacious and energetic expression than I had hitherto seen in the serene and passionless faces of the men. He brought me the tablet on which I had drawn the mode of my descent, and had also sketched the head of the horrible reptile that had scared me from my friend's corpse. Pointing to that part of the drawing, Taë put to me a few questions respecting the size and form of the monster, and the cave or chasm from which it had emerged. His interest in my answers seemed so grave as to divert him for a while from any curiosity as to myself or my antecedents. But to my great embarrassment, seeing how I was pledged to my host, he was just beginning to ask me where I came from, when Zee fortunately entered, and, over-hearing him, said, "Taë, give to our guest any in-formation he may desire, but ask none from him in return. To question him who he is, whence he comes, or wherefore he is here, would be a breach of the law which my father has laid down for this house."

"So be it," said Taë, pressing his hand to his heart; and from that moment, till the one in which I saw him last, this child, with whom I became very intimate, never once put to me any of the questions thus interdicted.

CHAPTER IX.

It was not for some time, and until, by repeated trances, if they are so to be called, my mind became better prepared to interchange ideas with my entertainers, and more fully to comprehend differences of manners and customs, at first too strange to my experience to be seized by my reason, that I was enabled to gather the following details respecting the origin and history of this subterranean population, as portion of one great family race called the Ana.

According to the earliest traditions, the remote progenitors of the race had once tenanted a world above the surface of that in which their descendants dwelt. Myths of that world were still preserved in their archives, and in those myths were legends of a vaulted dome in which the lamps were lighted by no human hand. But such legends were considered by most commentators as allegorical

fables. According to these traditions the earth itself, at the date to which the traditions ascend, was
not indeed in its infancy, but in the throes and
travail of transition from one form of development
to another, and subject to many violent revolutions
of nature. By one of such revolutions, that portion
of the upper world inhabited by the ancestors of
this race had been subjected to inundations, not
rapid, but gradual and uncontrollable, in which all,
save a scanty remnant, were submerged and per-
ished. Whether this be a record of our historical
and sacred Deluge, or of some earlier one contended for by geologists, I do not pretend to conjecture; though, according to the chronology of this
people as compared with that of Newton, it must
have been many thousands of years before the time
of Noah. On the other hand, the account of these
writers does not harmonise with the opinions most
in vogue among geological authorities, inasmuch as
it places the existence of a human race upon earth
at dates long anterior to that assigned to the terrestrial formation adapted to the introduction of
mammalia. A band of the ill-fated race, thus in-

vaded by the Flood, had, during the march of the
waters, taken refuge in caverns amidst the loftier
rocks, and, wandering through these hollows, they
lost sight of the upper world for ever. Indeed, the
whole face of the earth had been changed by this
great revulsion; land had been turned into sea—
sea into land. In the bowels of the inner earth
even now, I was informed as a positive fact, might
be discovered the remains of human habitation—
habitation not in huts and caverns, but in vast
cities whose ruins attest the civilisation of races
which flourished before the age of Noah, and are
not to be classified with those genera to which philosophy ascribes the use of flint and the ignorance
of iron.

The fugitives had carried with them the knowledge of the arts they had practised above ground
—arts of culture and civilisation. Their earliest
want must have been that of supplying below the
earth the light they had lost above it; and at no
time, even in the traditional period, do the races,
of which the one I now sojourned with formed a
tribe, seem to have been unacquainted with the art

of extracting light from gases, or manganese, or pe-
troleum. They had been accustomed in their
former state to contend with the rude forces of
nature; and indeed the lengthened battle they had
fought with their conqueror Ocean, which had taken
centuries in its spread, had quickened their skill in
curbing waters into dikes and channels. To this
skill they owed their preservation in their new
abode. "For many generations," said my host, with
a sort of contempt and horror, "these primitive
forefathers are said to have degraded their rank
and shortened their lives by eating the flesh of animals, many varieties of which had, like themselves,
escaped the Deluge, and sought shelter in the hollows of the earth; other animals, supposed to be
unknown to the upper world, those hollows themselves produced."

When what we should term the historical age
emerged from the twilight of tradition, the Ana
were already established in different communities
and had attained to a degree of civilisation very
analogous to that which the more advanced nations
above the earth now enjoy. They were familiar

with most of our mechanical inventions, including
the application of steam as well as gas. The communities were in fierce competition with each other.
They had their rich and their poor; they had orators and conquerors; they made war either for a
domain or an idea. Though the various states
acknowledged various forms of government, free
institutions were beginning to preponderate; popular
assemblies increased in power; republics soon became general; the democracy to which the most
enlightened European politicians look forward as
the extreme goal of political advancement, and
which still prevailed among other subterranean races,
whom they despised as barbarians, the loftier family
of Ana, to which belonged the tribe I was visiting
looked back to as one of the crude and ignorant
experiments which belong to the infancy of political
science. It was the age of envy and hate, of fierce
passions, of constant social changes more or less
violent, of strife between classes, of war between
state and state. This phase of society lasted, however, for some ages, and was finally brought to a
close, at least among the nobler and more intel-

lectual populations, by the gradual discovery of the
latent powers stored in the all-permeating fluid
which they denominate Vril.

According to the account I received from Zee,
who, as an erudite professor in the College of
Sages, had studied such matters more diligently
than any other member of my host's family, this
fluid is capable of being raised and disciplined into
the mightiest agency over all forms of matter,
animate or inanimate. It can destroy like the flash
of lightning; yet, differently applied, it can re-
plenish or invigorate life, heal, and preserve, and
on it they chiefly rely for the cure of disease, or
rather for enabling the physical organisation to
re-establish the due equilibrium of its natural
powers, and thereby to cure itself. By this agency
they rend way through the most solid substances,
and open valleys for culture through the rocks of
their subterranean wilderness. From it they extract the light which supplies their lamps, finding it
steadier, softer, and healthier than the other inflammable materials they had formerly used.

But the effects of the alleged discovery of the

means to direct the more terrible force of vril
were chiefly remarkable in their influence upon
social polity. As these effects became familiarly
known and skilfully administered, war between the
Vril-discoverers ceased, for they brought the art of
destruction to such perfection as to annul all
superiority in numbers, discipline, or military skill.
The fire lodged in the hollow of a rod directed by
the hand of a child could shatter the strongest
fortress, or cleave its burning way from the van to
the rear of an embattled host. If army met army,
and both had command of this agency, it could be
but to the annihilation of each. The age of war
was therefore gone, but with the cessation of war
other effects bearing upon the social state soon
became apparent. Man was so completely at the
mercy of man, each whom he encountered being
able, if so willing, to slay him on the instant, that
all notions of government by force gradually vanished from political systems and forms of law. It
is only by force that vast communities, dispersed
through great distances of space, can be kept together; but now there was no longer either the

necessity of self-preservation or the pride of aggrandisement to make one state desire to preponderate in population over another.

The Vril-discoverers thus, in the course of a
few generations, peacefully split into communities
of moderate size. The tribe amongst which I had
fallen was limited to 12,000 families. Each tribe
occupied a territory sufficient for all its wants, and
at stated periods the surplus population departed
to seek a realm of its own. There appeared no
necessity for any arbitrary selection of these
emigrants; there was always a sufficient number
who volunteered to depart.

These subdivided states, petty if we regard
either territory or population,—all appertained to
one vast general family. They spoke the same
language, though the dialects might slightly differ.
They intermarried; they maintained the same
general laws and customs; and so important a
bond between these several communities was the
knowledge of vril and the practice of its agencies,
that the word A-Vril was synonymous with civilisation; and Vril-ya, signifying "The Civilised Na-

tions," was the common name by which the communities employing the uses of vril distinguished
themselves from such of the Ana as were yet in a
state of barbarism.

The government of the tribe of Vril-ya I am
treating of was apparently very complicated, really
very simple. It was based upon a principle recognised in theory, though little carried out in
practice, above ground—viz., that the object of
all systems of philosophical thought tends to the
attainment of unity, or the ascent through all intervening labyrinths to the simplicity of a single
first cause or principle. Thus in politics, even
republican writers have agreed that a benevolent
autocracy would insure the best administration, if
there were any guarantees for its continuance, or
against its gradual abuse of the powers accorded
to it. This singular community elected therefore
a single supreme magistrate styled Tur; he held
his office nominally for life, but he could seldom
be induced to retain it after the first approach of
old age. There was indeed in this society nothing
to induce any of its members to covet the cares

5*

of office. No honours, no insignia of higher rank, were assigned to it. The supreme magistrate was not distinguished from the rest by superior habitation or revenue. On the other hand, the duties awarded to him were marvellously light and easy, requiring no preponderant degree of energy or intelligence. There being no apprehensions of war, there were no armies to maintain; being no government of force, there was no police to appoint and direct. What we call crime was utterly unknown to the Vril-ya; and there were no courts of criminal justice. The rare instances of civil disputes were referred for arbitration to friends chosen by either party, or decided by the Council of Sages, which will be described later. There were no professional lawyers; and indeed their laws were but amicable conventions, for there was no power to enforce laws against an offender who carried in his staff the power to destroy his judges. There were customs and regulations to compliance with which, for several ages, the people had tacitly habituated themselves; or if in any instance an individual felt such compliance hard, he quitted the community and went elsewhere. There was, in fact, quietly established amid this state, much the same compact that is found in our private families, in which we virtually say to any independent grown-up member of the family whom we receive and entertain, "Stay or go, according as our habits and regulations suit or displease you." But though there were no laws such as we call laws, no race above ground is so law-observing. Obedience to the rule adopted by the community has become as much an instinct as if it were implanted by nature. Even in every household the head of it makes a regulation for its guidance, which is never resisted nor even cavilled at by those who belong to the family. They have a proverb, the pithiness of which is much lost in this paraphrase, "No happiness without order, no order without authority, no authority without unity." The mildness of all government among them, civil or domestic, may be signalised by their idiomatic expressions for such terms as illegal or forbidden—viz., "It is requested not to do so-and-so." Poverty among the Ana is as unknown as crime; not that property is held in common, or that all are equals in the extent of their possessions or the size and luxury of their habitations: but there being no difference of rank or position between the grades of wealth or the choice of occupations, each pursues his own inclinations without creating envy or vying; some like a modest, some a more splendid kind of life; each makes himself happy in his own way. Owing to this absence of competition, and the limit placed on the population, it is difficult for a family to fall into distress; there are no hazardous speculations, no emulators striving for superior wealth and rank. No doubt, in each settlement all originally had the same proportions of land dealt out to them; but some, more adventurous than others, had extended their possessions farther into the bordering wilds, or had improved into richer fertility the produce of their fields, or entered into commerce or trade. Thus, necessarily, some had grown richer than others, but none had become absolutely poor, or wanting anything which their tastes desired. If they did so, it was always in

their power to migrate, or at the worst to apply,
without shame and with certainty of aid, to the
rich; for all the members of the community
considered themselves as brothers of one affectionate and united family. More upon this head will
be treated of incidentally as my narrative proceeds.

The chief care of the supreme magistrate was
to communicate with certain active departments
charged with the administration of special details.
The most important and essential of such details
was that connected with the due provision of light.
Of this department my host, Aph-Lin, was the
chief. Another department, which might be called
the foreign, communicated with the neighbouring
kindred states, principally for the purpose of
ascertaining all new inventions; and to a third department, all such inventions and improvements in
machinery were committed for trial. Connected
with this department was the College of Sages—a
college especially favoured by such of the Ana as
were widowed and childless, and by the young unmarried females, amongst whom Zee was the most
active, and, if what we call renown or distinction

was a thing acknowledged by this people (which I
shall later show it is not), among the most renowned or distinguished. It is by the female Professors of this College that those studies which are
deemed of least use in practical life—as purely
speculative philosophy, the history of remote
periods, and such sciences as entomology, concho-
logy, &c.—are the more diligently cultivated. Zee,
whose mind, active as Aristotle's, equally embraced
the largest domains and the minutest details of
thought, had written two volumes on the parasite
insect that dwells amid the hairs of a tiger's* paw,
which work was considered the best authority on
that interesting subject. But the researches of the
sages are not confined to such subtle or elegant
studies. They comprise various others more important, and especially the properties of vril, to

* The animal here referred to has many points of difference from the
tiger of the upper world. It is larger, and with a broader paw, and still
more receding frontal. It haunts the sides of lakes and pools, and feeds
principally on fishes, though it does not object to any terrestrial animal of
inferior strength than comes in its way. It is becoming very scarce even
in the wild districts, where it is devoured by gigantic reptiles. I apprehend that it clearly belongs to the tiger species, since the parasite ani-
malcule found in its paw, like that found in the Asiatic tiger's, is a minia-
ture image of itself.

the perception of which their finer nervous organisation renders the female Professors eminently keen. It is out of this college that the Tur, or chief magistrate, selects Councillors, limited to three, in the rare instances in which novelty of event or circumstance perplexes his own judgment.

There are a few other departments of minor consequence, but all are carried on so noiselessly and quietly that the evidence of a government seems to vanish altogether, and social order to be as regular and unobtrusive as if it were a law of nature. Machinery is employed to an inconceivable extent in all the operations of labour within and without doors, and it is the unceasing object of the department charged with its administration to extend its efficiency. There is no class of labourers or servants, but all who are required to assist or control the machinery are found in the children, from the time they leave the care of their mothers to the marriageable age, which they place at sixteen for the Gy-ei (the females), twenty for the Ana (the males). These children are formed into bands and sections under

their own chiefs, each following the pursuits in
which he is most pleased, or for which he feels
himself most fitted. Some take to handicrafts, some
to agriculture, some to household work, and some
to the only services of danger to which the population is exposed; for the sole perils that threaten
this tribe are, first, from those occasional convulsions within the earth, to foresee and guard against
which tasks their utmost ingenuity—irruptions of
fire and water, the storms of subterranean winds
and escaping gases. At the borders of the domain,
and at all places where such peril might be
apprehended, vigilant inspectors are stationed with
telegraphic communication to the hall in which
chosen sages take it by turns to hold perpetual sit-
tings. These inspectors are always selected from
the elder boys approaching the age of puberty, and
on the principle that at that age observation is
more acute and the physical forces more alert than
at any other. The second service of danger, less
grave, is in the destruction of all creatures hostile
to the life, or the culture, or even the comfort, of
the Ana. Of these the most formidable are the

vast reptiles, of some of which antediluvian relics
are preserved in our museums, and certain gigantic
winged creatures, half bird, half reptile. These,
together with lesser wild animals, corresponding to
our tigers or venomous serpents, it is left to the
younger children to hunt and destroy; because,
according to the Ana, here ruthlessness is wanted,
and the younger a child the more ruthlessly he will
destroy. There is another class of animals in the
destruction of which discrimination is to be used,
and against which children of intermediate age are
appointed—animals that do not threaten the life of
man, but ravage the produce of his labour, varieties
of the elk and deer species, and a smaller creature
much akin to our rabbit, though infinitely more
destructive to crops, and much more cunning in its
mode of depredation. It is the first object of these
appointed infants, to tame the more intelligent of
such animals into respect for enclosures signalised
by conspicuous landmarks, as dogs are taught to
respect a larder, or even to guard the master's
property. It is only where such creatures are found
untamable to this extent that they are destroyed.

Life is never taken away for food or for sport, and
never spared where untamably inimical to the Ana.
Concomitantly with these bodily services and tasks,
the mental education of the children goes on till
boyhood ceases. It is the general custom, then, to
pass through a course of instruction at the College
of Sages, in which, besides more general studies,
the pupil receives special lessons in such vocation
or direction of intellect as he himself selects. Some,
however, prefer to pass this period of probation in
travel, or to emigrate, or to settle down at once
into rural or commercial pursuits. No force is put
upon individual inclination.

———

CHAPTER X.

THE word Ana (pronounced broadly *Arna*) cor-
responds with our plural *men;* An (pronounced
Arn), the singular, with *man.* The word for woman
is Gy (pronounced hard, as in Guy); it forms itself
into Gy-ei for the plural, but the G becomes soft
in the plural, like Jy-ei. They have a proverb to
the effect that this difference in pronunciation is
symbolical, for that the female sex is soft col-
lectively, but hard to deal with in the individual.
The Gy-ei are in the fullest enjoyment of all the
rights of equality with males, for which certain philosophers above ground contend.

In childhood they perform the offices of work
and labour impartially with the boys; and, indeed,
in the earlier age appropriated to the destruction
of animals irreclaimably hostile, the girls are fre-
quently preferred, as being by constitution more
ruthless under the influence of fear or hate. In

the interval between infancy and the marriageable
age familiar intercourse between the sexes is suspended. At the marriageable age it is renewed,
never with worse consequences than those which
attend upon marriage. All·arts and vocations allotted to the one sex are open to the other, and
the Gy-ei arrogate to themselves a superiority in
all those abstruse and mystical branches of reasoning, for which they say the Ana are unfitted by a
duller sobriety of understanding, or the routine of
their matter-of-fact occupations, just as young ladies
in our own world constitute themselves authorities
in the subtlest points of theological doctrine, for
which few men, actively engaged in worldly business, have sufficient learning or refinement of intellect. Whether owing to early training in gym-
nastic exercises or to their constitutional organisation, the Gy-ei are usually superior to the Ana in
physical strength (an important element in the consideration and maintenance of female rights). They
attain to loftier stature, and amid their rounder
proportions are embedded sinews and muscles as
hardy as those of the other sex. Indeed they assert

that, according to the original laws of nature, females were intended to be larger than males, and maintain this dogma by reference to the earliest formations of life in insects, and in the most ancient family of the vertebrata — viz., fishes — in both of which the females are generally large enough to make a meal of their consorts if they so desire. Above all, the Gy-ei have a readier and more concentred power over that mysterious fluid or agency which contains the element of destruction, with a larger portion of that sagacity which comprehends dissimulation. Thus they can not only defend themselves against all aggressions from the males, but could, at any moment when he least suspected his danger, terminate the existence of an offending spouse. To the credit of the Gy-ei no instance of their abuse of this awful superiority in the art of destruction is on record for several ages. The last that occurred in the community I speak of appears (according to their chronology) to have been about two thousand years ago. A Gy, then, in a fit of jealousy, slew her husband; and this abominable act inspired such terror among the

males that they emigrated in a body and left all
the Gy-ei to themselves. The history runs that the
widowed Gy-ei, thus reduced to despair, fell upon
the murderess when in her sleep (and therefore un-
armed), and killed her, and then entered into a
solemn obligation amongst themselves to abrogate
for ever the exercise of their extreme conjugal
powers, and to inculcate the same obligation for
ever and ever on their female children. By this
conciliatory process, a deputation despatched to the
fugitive consorts succeeded in persuading many to
return, but those who did return were mostly the
elder ones. The younger, either from too craven a
doubt of their consorts, or too high an estimate of
their own merits, rejected all overtures, and, re-
maining in other communities, were caught up
there by other mates, with whom perhaps they were
no better off. But the loss of so large a portion of
the male youth operated as a salutary warning on
the Gy-ei, and confirmed them in the pious re-
solution to which they had pledged themselves.
Indeed it is now popularly considered that, by
long hereditary disuse, the Gy-ei have lost both the

aggressive and the defensive superiority over the
Ana which they once possessed, just as in the inferior animals above the earth many peculiarities in
their original formation, intended by nature for
their protection, gradually fade or become inopera-
tive when not needed under altered circumstances.
I should be sorry, however, for any An who induced a Gy to make the experiment whether he or
she were the stronger.

From the incident I have narrated, the Ana date
certain alterations in the marriage customs, tending,
perhaps, somewhat to the advantage of the male.
They now bind themselves in wedlock only for
three years; at the end of each third year either
male or female can divorce the other and is free
to marry again. At the end of ten years the An
has the privilege of taking a second wife, allowing
the first to retire if she so please. These regulations are for the most part a dead letter; divorces
and polygamy are extremely rare, and the marriage
state now seems singularly happy and serene among
this astonishing people;—the Gy-ei, notwithstanding their boastful superiority in physical strength

and intellectual abilities, being much curbed into
gentle manners by the dread of separation or of a
second wife, and the Ana being very much 'the
creatures of custom, and not, except upder great
aggravation, liking to exchange for hazardous
novelties faces and manners to which they are re-
conciled by habit. But there is one privilege the
Gy-ei carefully retain, and the desire for which
perhaps forms the secret motive of most lady as-
serters of woman rights above ground. They claim
the privilege, here usurped by men, of proclaiming
their love and urging their suit; in other words, of
being the wooing party rather than the wooed.
Such a phenomenon as an old maid does not exist
among the Gy-ei. Indeed it is very seldom that a
Gy does not secure any An upon whom she sets
her heart, if his affections be not strongly engaged
elsewhere. However coy, reluctant, and prudish,
the male she courts may prove at first, yet her per-
severance, her ardour, her persuasive powers, her
command over the mystic agencies of vril, are
pretty sure to run down his neck into what we call
"the fatal noose." Their argument for the reversal

of that relationship of the sexes which the blind
tyranny of man has established on the surface of
the earth, appears cogent, and is advanced with a
frankness which might well be commended to im-
partial consideration. They say, that of the two
the female is by nature of a more loving disposi-
tion than the male—that love occupies a larger
space in her thoughts, and is more essential to her
happiness, and that therefore she ought to be the
wooing party; that otherwise the male is a shy and
dubitant creature—that he has often a selfish predilection for the single state—that he often pretends
to misunderstand tender glances and delicate hints
—that, in short, he must be resolutely pursued and
captured. They add, moreover, that unless the Gy
can secure the An of her choice, and one whom
she would not select out of the whole world becomes her mate, she is not only less happy than
she otherwise would be, but she is not so good a
being, that her qualities of heart are not sufficiently
developed; whereas the An is a creature that less
lastingly concentrates his affections on one object;
that if he cannot get the Gy whom he prefers he

6*

easily reconciles himself to another Gy; and, finally,
that at the worst, if he is loved and taken care of,
it is less necessary to the welfare of his existence
that he should love as well as be loved; he grows
contented with his creature comforts, and the many
occupations of thought which he creates for himself.

Whatever may be said as to this reasoning, the
system works well for the male; for being thus sure
that he is truly and ardently loved, and that the
more coy and reluctant he shows himself, the more
the determination to secure him increases, he
generally contrives to make his consent dependent
on such conditions as he thinks the best calculated
to insure, if not a blissful, at least a peaceful life.
Each individual An has his own hobbies, his own
ways, his own predilections, and, whatever they
may be, he demands a promise of full and un-
restrained concession to them. This, in the pursuit
of her object, the Gy readily promises; and as the
characteristic of this extraordinary people is an im-
plicit veneration for truth, and her word once given
is never broken even by the giddiest Gy, the con-

ditions stipulated for are religiously observed. In fact, notwithstanding all their abstract rights and powers, the Gy-ei are the most amiable, conciliatory, and submissive wives I have ever seen even in the happiest households above ground. It is an aphorism among them, that "where a Gy loves it is her pleasure to obey." It will be observed that in the relationship of the sexes I have spoken only of marriage, for such is the moral perfection to which this community has attained, that any illicit connection is as little possible amongst them as it would be to a couple of linnets during the time they agreed to live in pairs.

CHAPTER XL

NOTHING had more perplexed me in seeking to reconcile my sense to the existence of regions extending below the surface of the earth, and habitable by beings, if dissimilar from, still, in all material points of organism, akin to those in the upper world, than the contradiction thus presented to the doctrine in which, I believe, most geologists and philosophers concur—viz., that though with us the sun is the great source of heat, yet the deeper we go beneath the crust of the earth, the greater is the increasing heat, being, it is said, found in the ratio of a degree for every foot, commencing from fifty feet below the surface. But though the domains of the tribe I speak of were, on the higher ground, so comparatively near to the surface, that I could account for a temperature, therein, suitable to organic life, yet even the ravines and valleys of that realm were much less hot than philosophers would deem

possible at such a depth — certainly not warmer
than the south of France, or at least of Italy. And
according to all the accounts I received, vast tracts
immeasurably deeper beneath the surface, and in
which one might have thought only salamanders
could exist, were inhabited by innumerable races
organised like ourselves. I cannot pretend in any
way to account for a fact which is so at variance
with the recognised laws of science, nor could Zee
much help me towards a solution of it. She did
but conjecture that sufficient allowance had not
been made by our philosophers for the extreme
porousness of the interior earth—the vastness of its
cavities and irregularities, which served to create
free currents of air and frequent winds—and for
the various modes in which heat is evaporated and
thrown off. She allowed, however, that there was
a depth at which the heat was deemed to be intolerable to such organised life as was known to
the experience of the Vril-ya, though their philosophers believed that even in such places life of
some kind, life sentient, life intellectual, would be
found abundant and thriving, could the philo-

sophers penetrate to it. "Wherever the All-Good
builds," said she, "there, be sure, He places inhabitants. He loves not empty dwellings." She
added, however, that many changes in temperature
and climate had been effected by the skill of the
Vril-ya, and that the agency of vril had been suc-
cessfully employed in such changes. She described
a subtle and life-giving medium called Lai, which I
suspect to be identical with the ethereal oxygen of
Dr. Lewins, wherein work all the correlative forces
united under the name of vril; and contended that
wherever this medium could be expanded, as it
were, sufficiently for the various agencies of vril to
have ample play, a temperature congenial to the
highest forms of life could be secured. She said
also, that it was the belief of their naturalists that
flowers and vegetation had been produced originally
(whether developed from seeds borne from the surface of the earth in the earlier convulsions of
nature, or imported by the tribes that first sought
refuge in cavernous hollows) through the operations
of the light constantly brought to bear on them,
and the gradual improvement in culture. She said

also, that since the vril light had superseded all other light-giving bodies, the colours of flower and foliage had become more brilliant, and vegetation had acquired larger growth.

Leaving these matters to the consideration of those better competent to deal with them, I must now devote a few pages to the very interesting questions connected with the language of the Vril-ya.

———

CHAPTER XII

THE language of the Vril-ya is peculiarly interesting, because it seems to me to exhibit with
great clearness the traces of the three main transi-
tions through which language passes in attaining to
perfection of form.

One of the most illustrious of recent philolo-
gists, Max Müller, in arguing for the analogy
between the strata of language and the strata of
the earth, lays down this absolute dogma: "No
language can, by any possibility, be inflectional
without having passed through the agglutinative
and isolating stratum. No language can be agglutinative without clinging with its roots to the
underlying stratum of isolation."—'On the Stratification of Language,' p. 20.

Taking then the Chinese language as the best
existing type of the original isolating stratum, "as
the faithful photograph of man in his leading-strings

trying the muscles of his mind, groping his way, and so delighted with his first successful grasps that he repeats them again and again,"*—we have, in the language of the Vril-ya, still "clinging with its roots to the underlying stratum," the evidences of the original isolation. It abounds in monosyllables, which are the foundations of the language. The transition into the agglutinative form marks an epoch that must have gradually extended through ages, the written literature of which has only survived in a few fragments of symbolical mythology and certain pithy sentences which have passed into popular proverbs. With the extant literature of the Vril-ya the inflectional stratum commences. No doubt at that time there must have operated concurrent causes, in the fusion of races by some dominant people, and the rise of some great literary phenomena by which the form of language became arrested and fixed. As the inflectional stage prevailed over the agglutinative, it is surprising to see how much more boldly the original roots of the language project from the surface that conceals

* Max Müller, 'Stratification of Language.' p. 13.

them. In the old fragments and proverbs of the
preceding stage the monosyllables which compose
those roots vanish amidst words of enormous length,
comprehending whole sentences from which no one
part can be disentangled from the other and employed separately. But when the inflectional form
of language became so far advanced as to have its
scholars and grammarians, they seem to have united
in extirpating all such polysynthetical or polysyllabic
monsters, as devouring invaders of the aboriginal
forms. Words beyond three syllables became pro-
scribed as barbarous, and in proportion as the language grew thus simplified it increased in strength,
in dignity, and in sweetness. Though now very
compressed in sound, it gains in clearness by that
compression. By a single letter, according to its
position, they contrive to express all that with
civilised nations in our upper world it takes the
waste, sometimes of syllables, sometimes of sentences,
to express. Let me here cite one or two instances:
An (which I will translate man), Ana (men); the
letter s is with them a letter implying multitude,
according to where it is placed; Sana means man-

kind; Ansa, a multitude of men. The prefix of
certain letters in their alphabet invariably denotes
compound significations. For instance, Gl (which
with them is a single letter, as *th* is a single letter
with the Greeks) at the commencement of a word
infers an assemblage or union of things, sometimes
kindred, sometimes dissimilar—as Oon, a house;
Gloon, a town (*i. e.*, an assemblage of houses). Ata
is sorrow; Glata, a public calamity. Aur-an is the
health or wellbeing of a man; Glauran, the wellbeing of the state, the good of the community; and
a word constantly in their mouths is A-glauran,
which denotes their political creed—viz., that "the first
principle of a community is the good of all." Aub
is invention; Sila, a tone in music. Glaubsila, as
uniting the ideas of invention and of musical intona-
tion, is the classical word for poetry—abbreviated,
in ordinary conversation, to Glaubs. Na, which
with them is, like Gl, but a single letter, always,
when an initial, implies something antagonistic to
life or joy or comfort, resembling in this the Aryan
root Nak, expressive of perishing or destruction.
Nax is darkness; Narl, death; Naria, sin or evil

Nas—an uttermost condition of sin and evil—
corruption. In writing, they deem it irreverent to
express the Supreme Being by any special name.
He is symbolised by what may be termed the
hieroglyphic of a pyramid, ∧. In prayer they
address Him by a name which they deem too sacred
to confide to a stranger, and I know it not. In
conversation they generally use a periphrastic
epithet, such as the All-Good. The letter V, symbolical of the inverted pyramid, where it is an
initial, nearly always denotes excellence or power;
as Vril, of which I have said so much; Veed, an
immortal spirit; Veedya, immortality; Koom, pronounced like the Welsh Cwm, denotes something
of hollowness. Koom itself is a profound hollow,
metaphorically a cavern; Koom-in, a hole; Zi-koom,
a valley; Koom-zi, vacancy or void; Bodh-koom,
ignorance (literally, knowledge-void). Koom-Posh
is their name for the government of the many, or
the ascendancy of the most ignorant or hollow.
Posh is an almost untranslatable idiom, implying,
as the reader will see later, contempt. The closest
rendering I can give to it is our slang term,

"bosh;" and thus Koom-Posh may be loosely
rendered "Hollow-Bosh." But when Democracy or
Koom-Posh degenerates from popular ignorance
into that popular passion or ferocity which precedes
its decease, as (to cite illustrations from the upper
world) during the French Reign of Terror, or for
the fifty years of the Roman Republic preceding the
ascendancy of Augustus, their name for that state
of things is Glek-Nas. Ek is strife — Glek, the universal strife. Nas, as I before said, is corruption
or rot; thus Glek-Nas may be construed, "the
universal strife-rot." Their compounds are very
expressive; thus, Bodh being knowledge, and Too
a participle that implies the action of cautiously
approaching, — Too-bodh is their word for Philosophy; Pah is a contemptuous exclamation analogous to our idiom, "stuff and nonsense;" Pah-
bodh (literally, stuff-and-nonsense-knowledge) is
their term for futile or false philosophy, and is
applied to a species of metaphysical or speculative
ratiocination formerly in vogue, which consisted in
making inquiries that could not be answered, and
were not worth making; such, for instance, as,

"Why does an An have five toes to his feet instead
of four or six? Did the first An, created by the
All-Good, have the same number of toes as his descendants? In the form by which an An will be
recognised by his friends in the future state of
being, will he retain any toes at all, and, if so, will
they be material toes or spiritual toes?" I take
these illustrations of Pah-bodh, not in irony or jest,
but because the very inquiries I name formed the
subject of controversy by the latest cultivators of
that 'science'—4000 years ago.

In the declension of nouns I was informed that
anciently there were eight cases (one more than in
the Sanskrit Grammar); but the effect of time has
been to reduce these cases, and multiply, instead
of these varying terminations, explanatory preposi-
tions. At present, in the Grammar submitted to
my study, there were four cases to nouns, three
having varying terminations, and the fourth a differing prefix.

	SINGULAR.		PLURAL.	
Nom.	An,	Man.	Nom.	Ana,	Men.
Dat.	Ano,	to Man.	Dat.	Anoi,	to Men.
Ac.	Ana,	Man.	Ac.	Ananda,	Men.
Voc.	Hil-An,	O Man.	Voc.	Hil-Ananda,	O Men.

In the elder inflectional literature the dual form existed—it has long been obsolete.

The genitive case with them is also obsolete; the dative supplies its place: they say the House *to* a Man, instead of the House *of* a Man. When used (sometimes in poetry), the genitive in the termination is the same as the nominative; so is the ablative, the preposition that marks it being a prefix or suffix at option, and generally decided by ear, according to the sound of the noun. It will be observed that the prefix Hil marks the vocative case. It is always retained in addressing another, except in the most intimate domestic relations; its omission would be considered rude: just as in our old forms of speech in addressing a king it would have been deemed disrespectful to say "King," and reverential to say "O King." In fact, as they have no titles of honour, the vocative adjuration supplies the place of a title, and is given impartially to all. The prefix Hil enters into the composition of words that imply distant communications, as Hil-ya, to travel.

In the conjugation of their verbs, which is much

too lengthy a subject to enter on here, the auxiliary verb Ya, "to go," which plays so considerable part in the Sanskrit, appears and performs a kindred office, as if it were a radical in some language from which both had descended. But another auxiliary of opposite signification also accompanies it and shares its labours—viz., Zi, to stay or repose. Thus Ya enters into the future tense, and Zi in the preterite of all verbs requiring auxiliaries. Yam, I go —Yiam, I may go—Yani-ya, I shall go (literally, I go to go)—Zampoo-yan, I have gone (literally, I rest from gone). Ya, as a termination, implies by analogy, progress, movement, efflorescence. Zi, as a terminal, denotes fixity, sometimes in a good sense, sometimes in a bad, according to the word with which it is coupled. Iva-zi, eternal goodness; Nan-zi, eternal evil. Poo (from) enters as a prefix to words that denote repugnance, or things from which we ought to be averse. Poo-pra, disgust; Poo-naria, falsehood, the vilest kind of evil. Poosh or Posh I have already confessed to be untranslatable literally. It is an expression of contempt not unmixed with pity. This radical seems to have originated from inherent sympathy between the labial effort and the sentiment that impelled it, Poo being an utterance in which the breath is exploded from the lips with more or less vehemence. On the other hand, Z, when an initial, is with them a sound in which the breath is sucked inward, and thus Zu, pronounced Zoo (which in their language is one letter), is the ordinary prefix to words that signify something that attracts, pleases, touches the heart—as Zummer, lover; Zutze, love; Zuzulia, delight. This indrawn sound of Z seems indeed naturally appropriate to fondness. Thus, even in our language, mothers say to their babies, in defiance of grammar, "Zoo darling;" and I have heard a learned professor at Boston call his wife (he had been only married a month) "Zoo little pet."

I cannot quit this subject, however, without observing by what slight changes in the dialects favoured by different tribes of the same race, the original signification and beauty of sounds may become confused and deformed. Zee told me with much indignation that Zummer (lover) which, in the way she uttered it, seemed slowly taken down

7*

to the very depths of her heart, was, in some not
very distant communities of the Vril-ya, vitiated
into the half-hissing, half-nasal, wholly disagreeable,
sound of Sübber. I thought to myself it only
wanted the introduction of *n* before *u* to render it
into an English word significant of the last quality
an amorous Gy would desire in her Zummer.

I will but mention another peculiarity in this
language which gives equal force and brevity to its
forms of expressions.

A is with them, as with us, the first letter of
the alphabet, and is often used as a prefix word by
itself to convey a complex idea of sovereignty or
chiefdom, or presiding principle. For instance, Iva
is goodness; Diva, goodness and happiness united;
A-Diva is unerring and absolute truth. I have already noticed the value of A in A-glauran, so, in
vril (to whose properties they trace their present
state of civilisation), A-vril, denotes, as I have said,
civilisation itself.

The philologist will have seen from the above
how much the language of the Vril-ya is akin to
the Aryan or Indo-Germanic; but, like all languages,

it contains words and forms in which transfers from
very opposite sources of speech have been taken.
The very title of Tur, which they give to their
supreme magistrate, indicates theft from a tongue
akin to the Turanian. They say themselves that
this is a foreign word borrowed from a title which
their historical records show to have been borne
by the chief of a nation with whom the ancestors
of the Vril-ya were, in very remote periods, on
friendly terms, but which has long become extinct,
and they say that when, after the discovery of vril,
they remodelled their political institutions, they ex-
pressly adopted a title taken from an extinct race
and a dead language for that of their chief magistrate, in order to avoid all titles for that office with
which they had previous associations.

Should life be spared to me, I may collect into
systematic form such knowledge as I acquired of
this language during my sojourn amongst the Vril-
ya. But what I have already said will perhaps
suffice to show to genuine philological students that
a language which, preserving so many of the roots
in the aboriginal form, and clearing from the im-

mediate, but transitory, polysynthetical stage so
many rude incumbrances, has attained to such a
union of simplicity and compass in its final inflectional forms, must have been the gradual work
of countless ages and many varieties of mind; that
it contains the evidence of fusion between congenial
races, and necessitated, in arriving at the shape of
which I have given examples, the continuous culture of a highly thoughtful people.

That, nevertheless, the literature which belongs
to this language is a literature of the past; that the
present felicitous state of society at which the Ana
have attained forbids the progressive cultivation
of literature, especially in the two main divisions of
fiction and history,—I shall have occasion to show
later.

CHAPTER XIII.

THIS people have a religion, and, whatever may
be said against it, at least it has these strange
peculiarities: firstly, that they all believe in the
creed they profess; secondly, that they all practise
the precepts which the creed inculcates. They
unite in the worship of the one divine Creator and
Sustainer of the universe. They believe that it is
one of the properties of the all-permeating agency
of vril, to transmit to the well-spring of life and
intelligence every thought that a living creature can
conceive; and though they do not contend that the
idea of a Deity is innate, yet they say that the An
(man) is the only creature, so far as their observation of nature extends, to whom *the capacity of
conceiving that idea*, with all the trains of thought
which open out from it, is vouchsafed. They hold
that this capacity is a privilege that cannot have
been given in vain, and hence that prayer and

thanksgiving are acceptable to the divine Creator, and necessary to the complete development of the human creature. They offer their devotions both in private and public. Not being considered one of their species, I was not admitted into the building or temple in which the public worship is rendered; but I am informed that the service is exceedingly short, and unattended with any pomp of ceremony. It is a doctrine with the Vril-ya, that earnest devotion or complete abstraction from the actual world cannot, with benefit to itself, be maintained long at a stretch by the human mind, especially in public, and that all attempts to do so either lead to fanaticism or to hypocrisy. When they pray in private, it is when they are alone or with their young children.

They say that in ancient times there was a great number of books written upon speculations as to the nature of the Deity, and upon the forms of belief or worship supposed to be most agreeable to Him. But these were found to lead to such heated and angry disputations as not only to shake the peace of the community and divide families before

the most united, but in the course of discussing the
attributes of the Deity, the existence of the Deity
Himself became argued away, or, what was worse,
became invested with the passions and infirmities
of the human disputants. "For," said my host,
"since a finite being like an An cannot possibly
define the Infinite, so, when he endeavours to realise
an idea of the Divinity, he only reduces the Divinity
into an An like himself." During the later ages,
therefore, all theological speculations, though not
forbidden, have been so discouraged as to have
fallen utterly into disuse.

The Vril-ya unite in a conviction of a future
state, more felicitous and more perfect than the
present. If they have very vague notions of the
doctrine of rewards and punishments, it is perhaps
because they have no systems of rewards and
punishments among themselves, for there are no
crimes to punish, and their moral standard is so
even that no An among them is, upon the whole,
considered more virtuous than another. If one
excels, perhaps, in one virtue, another equally excels
in some other virtue; if one has his prevalent fault

or infirmity, so also another has his. In fact, in
their extraordinary mode of life, there are so few
temptations to wrong, that they are good (according to their notions of goodness) merely because
they live. They have some fanciful notions upon
the continuance of life, when once bestowed, even
in the vegetable world, as the reader will see in the
next chapter.

———————

CHAPTER XIV.

THOUGH, as I have said, the Vril-ya discourage all speculations on the nature of the Supreme Being, they appear to concur in a belief by which they think to solve that great problem of the existence of evil which has so perplexed the philosophy of the upper world. They hold that wherever He has once given life, with the perceptions of that life, however faint it be, as in a plant, the life is never destroyed; it passes into new and improved forms, though not in this planet (differing therein from the ordinary doctrine of metempsychosis), and that the living thing retains the sense of identity, so that it connects its past life with its future, and is *conscious* of its progressive improvement in the scale of joy. For they say that, without this assumption, they cannot, according to the lights of human reason vouchsafed to them, discover the perfect justice which must be a constituent quality of the All-Wise

and the All-Good. Injustice, they say, can only
emanate from three causes: want of wisdom to perceive what is just, want of benevolence to desire,
want of power to fulfil it; and that each of these
three wants is incompatible in the All-Wise, the
All-Good, the All-Powerful. But that, while even
in this life, the wisdom, the benevolence, and the
power of the Supreme Being are sufficiently apparent to compel our recognition, the justice necessarily resulting from those attributes, absolutely
requires another life, not for man only, but for
every living thing of the inferior orders. That,
alike in the animal and the vegetable world, we see
one individual rendered, by circumstances beyond
its control, exceedingly wretched compared to its
neighbours—one only exists as the prey of another
—even a plant suffers from disease till it perishes
prematurely, while the plant next to it rejoices in
its vitality and lives out its happy life free from a
pang. That it is an erroneous analogy from human
infirmities to reply by saying that the Supreme
Being only acts by general laws, thereby making
his own secondary causes so potent as to mar the

essential kindness of the First Cause; and a still
meaner and more ignorant conception of the All-
Good, to dismiss with a brief contempt all consideration of justice for the myriad forms into
which He has infused life, and assume that justice
is only due to the single product of the An. There
is no small and no great in the eyes of the divine
Life-Giver. But once grant that nothing, however
humble, which feels that it lives and suffers, can
perish through the series of ages, that all its suffering here, if continuous from the moment of its
birth to that of its transfer to another form of being,
would be more brief compared with eternity than
the cry of the new-born is compared to the whole
life of a man; and once suppose that this living
thing retains its sense of identity when so transferred (for without that sense it could be aware of
no future being), and though, indeed, the fulfilment
of divine justice is removed from the scope of our
ken, yet we have a right to assume it to be uniform
and universal, and not varying and partial, as it
would be if acting only upon general secondary
laws; because such perfect justice flows of necessity

from perfectness of knowledge to conceive, perfectness of love to will, and perfectness of power to
complete it.

However fantastic this belief of the Vril-ya may
be, it tends perhaps to confirm politically the
systems of government which, admitting differing
degrees of wealth, yet establishes perfect equality
in rank, exquisite mildness in all relations and intercourse, and tenderness to all created things
which the good of the community does not require
them to destroy. And though their notion of com-
pensation to a tortured insect or a cankered flower
may seem to some of us a very wild crotchet, yet,
at least, it is not a mischievous one; and it may
furnish matter for no unpleasing reflection to think
that within the abysses of earth, never lit by a ray
from the material heavens, there should have penetrated so luminous a conviction of the ineffable
goodness of the Creator—so fixed an idea that the
general laws by which He acts cannot admit of any
partial injustice or evil, and therefore cannot be
comprehended without reference to their action
over all space and throughout all time. And since,

as I shall have occasion to observe later, the intellectual conditions and social systems of this subterranean race comprise and harmonise great, and
apparently antagonistic, varieties in philosophical
doctrine and speculation which have from time to
time been started, discussed, dismissed and have
re-appeared amongst thinkers or dreamers in the
upper world,—so I may perhaps appropriately con-
clude this reference to the belief of the Vril-ya
that self-conscious or sentient life once given is
indestructible among inferior creatures as well as
in man, by an eloquent passage from the work of
that eminent zoologist, Louis Agassiz, which I
have only just met with, many years after I had
committed to paper those recollections of the life
of the Vril-ya which I now reduce into something like arrangement and form: "The relations
which individual animals bear to one another are
of such a character that they ought long ago to
have been considered as sufficient proof that no
organised being could ever have been called into
existence by other agency than by the direct inter-
vention of a reflective mind. This argues strongly

in favour of the existence in every animal of an
immaterial principle similar to that which by its
excellence and superior endowments places man
so much above animals; yet the principle unques-
tionably exists, and whether it be called sense,
reason, or instinct, it presents in the whole range
of organised beings a series of phenomena closely
linked together, and upon it are based not only the
higher manifestations of the mind, but the very per-
manence of the specific differences which charac-
terise every organism. Most of the arguments in
favour of the immortality of man apply equally to
the permanency of this principle in other living
beings. May I not add that a future life in which
man would be deprived of that great source of
enjoyment and intellectual and moral improvement
which results from the contemplation of the harmonies of an organic world would involve a
lamentable loss? And may we not look to a spiritual concert of the combined worlds and *all* their
inhabitants in the presence of their Creator as the
highest conception of paradise?"—'*Essay on Clas-
sification,' sect. xvii. p.* 97-99.

CHAPTER XV.

KIND to me as I found all in this household, the young daughter of my host was the most considerate and thoughtful in her kindness. At her suggestion I laid aside the habiliments in which I had descended from the upper earth, and adopted the dress of the Vril-ya, with the exception of the artful wings which served them, when on foot, as a graceful mantle. But as many of the Vril-ya, when occupied in urban pursuits, did not wear these wings, this exception created no marked difference between myself and the race among which I sojourned, and I was thus enabled to visit the town without exciting unpleasant curiosity. Out of the household no one suspected that I had come from the upper world, and I was but regarded as one of some inferior and barbarous tribe whom Aph-Lin entertained as a guest.

The city was large in proportion to the territory round it, which was of no greater extent than many

an English or Hungarian nobleman's estate; but
the whole of it, to the verge of the rocks which
constituted its boundary, was cultivated to the
nicest degree, except where certain allotments of
mountain and pasture were humanely left free to
the sustenance of the harmless animals they had
tamed, though not for domestic use. So great is
their kindness towards these humbler creatures, that
a sum is devoted from the public treasury for the
purpose of deporting them to other Vril-ya communities willing to receive them (chiefly new colo-
nies), whenever they become too numerous for the
pastures allotted to them in their native place.
They do not, however, multiply to an extent com-
parable to the ratio at which, with us, animals bred
for slaughter, increase. It seems a law of nature
that animals not useful to man gradually recede
from the domains he occupies, or even become
extinct. It is an old custom of the various sovereign states amidst which the race of the Vril-ya
are distributed, to leave between each state a
neutral and uncultivated border-land. In the instance of the community I speak of, this tract, being

a ridge of savage rocks, was impassable by foot,
but was easily surmounted, whether by the wings
of the inhabitants or the air-boats, of which I shall
speak hereafter. Roads through it were also cut
for the transit of vehicles impelled by vril. These
intercommunicating tracts were always kept lighted,
and the expense thereof defrayed by a special tax,
to which all the communities comprehended in the
denomination of Vril-ya contribute in settled proportions. By these means a considerable commercial traffic with other states, both near and
distant, was carried on. The surplus wealth of this
special community was chiefly agricultural. The
community was also eminent for skill in constructing implements connected with the arts of hus-
bandry. In exchange for such merchandise it ob-
tained articles more of luxury than necessity. There
were few things imported on which they set a
higher price than birds taught to pipe artful tunes
in concert. These were brought from a great distance, and were marvellous for beauty of song and
plumage. I understood that extraordinary care was
taken by their breeders and teachers in selection,

8*

and that the species had wonderfully improved
during the last few years. I saw no other pet
animals among this community except some very
amusing and sportive creatures of the Batrachian
species, resembling frogs, but with very intelligent
countenances, which the children were fond of, and
kept in their private gardens. They appear to have
no animals akin to our dogs or horses, though that
learned naturalist, Zee, informed me that such
creatures had once existed in those parts, and might
now be found in regions inhabited by other races
than the Vril-ya. She said that they had gradually
disappeared from the more civilised world since the
discovery of vril, and the results attending that discovery, had dispensed with their uses. Machinery
and the invention of wings had superseded the
horse as a beast of burden; and the dog was no
longer wanted either for protection or the chase, as
it had been when the ancestors of the Vril-ya feared
the aggressions of their own kind, or hunted the
lesser animals for food. Indeed, however, so far as
the horse was concerned, this region was so rocky
that a horse could have been, there, of little use

either for pastime or burden. The only creature
they use for the latter purpose is a kind of large
goat which is much employed on farms. The
nature of the surrounding soil in these districts may
be said to have first suggested the invention of
wings and air-boats. The largeness of space, in
proportion to the rural territory occupied by the
city, was occasioned by the custom of surrounding
every house with a separate garden. The broad
main street, in which Aph-Lin dwelt, expanded into
a vast square, in which were placed the College of
Sages and all the public offices; a magnificent
fountain of the luminous fluid which I call naphtha
(I am ignorant of its real nature) in the centre.
All these public edifices have a uniform character
of massiveness and solidity. They reminded me of
the architectural pictures of Martin. Along the
upper stories of each ran a balcony, or rather a
terraced garden, supported by columns, filled with
flowering-plants, and tenanted by many kinds of
tame birds. From the square branched several
streets, all broad and brilliantly lighted, and ascend-
ing up the eminence on either side. In my excur-

sions in the town I was never allowed to go alone;
Aph-Lin or his daughter was my habitual companion. In this community the adult Gy is seen
walking with any young An as familiarly as if there
were no difference of sex.

The retail shops are not very numerous; the
persons who attend on a customer are all children
of various ages, and exceedingly intelligent and
courteous, but without the least touch of im-
portunity or cringing. The shopkeeper himself
might or might not be visible; when visible, he
seemed rarely employed on any matter connected
with his professional business; and yet he had
taken to that business from special liking to it,
and quite independently of his general sources of
fortune.

Some of the richest citizens in the community
kept such shops. As I have before said, no difference of rank is recognisable, and therefore all
occupations hold the same equal social status. An
An, of whom I bought my sandals, was the brother
of the Tur, or chief magistrate; and though his shop
was not larger than that of any bootmaker in Bond

Street or Broadway, he was said to be twice as rich as the Tur who dwelt in a palace. No doubt, however, he had some country-seat.

The Ana of the community are, on the whole, an indolent set of beings after the active age of childhood. Whether by temperament or philosophy, they rank repose among the chief blessings of life. Indeed, when you take away from a human being the incentives to action which are found in cupidity or ambition, it seems to me no wonder that he rests quiet.

In their ordinary movements they prefer the use of their feet to that of their wings. But for their sports or (to indulge in a bold misuse of terms) their public *promenades*, they employ the latter, also for the aerial dances I have described, as well as for visiting their country places, which are mostly placed on lofty heights; and, when still young, they prefer their wings, for travel into the other regions of the Ana, to vehicular conveyances.

Those who accustom themselves to flight can fly, if less rapidly than some birds, yet from twenty-five to thirty miles an hour, and keep up that rate

for five or six hours at a stretch. But the Ana
generally, on reaching middle age, are not fond of
rapid movements requiring violent exercise. Perhaps for this reason, as they hold a doctrine which
our own physicians will doubtless approve—viz,
that regular transpiration through the pores of the
skin is essential to health, they habitually use the
sweating-baths to which we give the name of
Turkish or Roman, succeeded by douches of perfumed waters. They have great faith in the salubri-
ous virtue of certain perfumes.

It is their custom also, at stated but rare periods,
perhaps four times a-year when in health, to use a
bath charged with vril.* They consider that this
fluid, sparingly used, is a great sustainer of life;
but used in excess, when in the normal state of
health, rather tends to reaction and exhausted
vitality. For nearly all their diseases, however, they
resort to it as the chief assistant to nature in throwing off the complaint.

* I once tried the effect of the vril bath. It was very similar in its
invigorating powers to that of the baths at Gastein, the virtues of which
are ascribed by many physicians to electricity; but though similar, the
effect of the vril bath was more lasting.

In their own way they are the most luxurious of people, but all their luxuries are innocent. They may be said to dwell in an atmosphere of music and fragrance. Every room has its mechanical contrivances for melodious sounds, usually tuned down to soft-murmured notes, which seem like sweet whispers from invisible spirits. They are too accustomed to these gentle sounds to find them a hindrance to conversation, nor, when alone, to reflection. But they have a notion that to breathe an air filled with continuous melody and perfume has necessarily an effect at once soothing and elevating upon the formation of character and the habits of thought. Though so temperate, and with total abstinence from other animal food than milk, and from all intoxicating drinks, they are delicate and dainty to an extreme in food and beverage; and in all their sports even the old exhibit a childlike gaiety. Happiness is the end at which they aim, not as the excitement of a moment, but as the prevailing condition of the entire existence; and regard for the happiness of each other is evinced by the exquisite amenity of their manners.

Their conformation of skull has marked differences from that of any known races in the upper world, though I cannot help thinking it a development, in the course of countless ages, of the Brachycephalic type of the Age of Stone in Lyell's 'Elements of Geology,' C. X., p. 113, as compared with the Dolichocephalic type of the beginning of the Age of Iron, correspondent with that now so prevalent amongst us, and called the Celtic type. It has the same comparative massiveness of forehead, not receding like the Celtic—the same even roundness in the frontal organs; but it is far loftier in the apex, and far less pronounced in the hinder cranial hemisphere where phrenologists place the animal organs. To speak as a phrenologist, the cranium common to the Vril-ya has the organs of weight, number, tune, form, order, causality, very largely developed; that of construction much more pronounced than that of ideality. Those which are called the moral organs, such as conscientiousness and benevolence, are amazingly full; amativeness and combativeness are both small; adhesiveness large; the organ of destructiveness (i.e., of de-

termined clearance of intervening obstacles) immense, but less than that of benevolence; and their
philoprogenitiveness takes rather the character of
compassion and tenderness to things that need aid
or protection than of the animal love of offspring.
I never met with one person deformed or misshapen.
The beauty of their countenances is not only in
symmetry of feature, but in a smoothness of surface,
which continues without line or wrinkle to the
extreme of old age, and a serene sweetness of expression, combined with that majesty which seems
to come from consciousness of power and the
freedom of all terror, physical or moral. It is that
very sweetness, combined with that majesty, which
inspired in a beholder like myself, accustomed to
strive with the passions of mankind, a sentiment of
humiliation, of awe, of dread. It is such an expression as a painter might give to a demi-god, a
genius, an angel. The males of the Vril-ya are
entirely beardless; the Gy-ei sometimes, in old age,
develop a small moustache.

I was surprised to find that the colour of their
skin was not uniformly that which I had remarked
in those individuals whom I had first encountered,

—some being much fairer, and even with blue
eyes, and hair of a deep golden auburn, though
still of complexions warmer or richer in tone than
persons in the north of Europe.

I was told that this admixture of colouring arose
from intermarriage with other and more distant
tribes of the Vril-ya, who, whether by the accident
of climate or early distinction of race, were of
fairer hues than the tribes of which this community
formed one. It was considered that the dark-red
skin showed the most ancient family of Ana; but
they attached no sentiment of pride to that antiquity, and, on the contrary, believed their present
excellence of breed came from frequent crossing
with other families differing, yet akin; and they
encourage such intermarriages, always provided
that it be with the Vril-ya nations. Nations which,
not conforming their manners and institutions to
those of the Vril-ya, nor indeed held capable of
acquiring the powers over the vril agencies which
it had taken them generations to attain and transmit,
were regarded with more disdain than citizens of
New York regard the negroes.

I learned from Zee, who had more lore in all

matters than any male with whom I was brought
into familiar converse, that the superiority of the
Vril-ya was supposed to have originated in the in-
tensity of their earlier struggles against obstacles
in nature amidst the localities in which they had
first settled. "Wherever," said Zee, moralising,
"wherever goes on that early process in the history
of civilisation, by which life is made a struggle,
in which the individual has to put forth all his
powers to compete with his fellow, we invariably
find this result—viz., since in the competition a
vast number must perish, nature selects for preservation only the strongest specimens. With our
race, therefore, even before the discovery of vril,
only the highest organisations were preserved; and
there is among our ancient books a legend, once
popularly believed, that we were driven from a
region that seems to denote the world you come
from, in order to perfect our condition and attain
to the purest elimination of our species by the
severity of the struggles our forefathers underwent;
and that, when our education shall become finally
completed, we are destined to return to the upper

world, and supplant all the inferior races now existing therein."

Aph-Lin and Zee often conversed with me in private upon the political and social conditions of that upper world, in which Zee so philosophically assumed that the inhabitants were to be exter-minated one day or other by the advent of the Vril-ya. They found in my accounts,—in which I continued to do all I could (without launching into falsehoods so positive that they would have been easily detected by the shrewdness of my listeners) to present our powers and ourselves in the most flattering point of view,—perpetual subjects of comparison between our most civilised populations and the meaner subterranean races which they considered hopelessly plunged in barbarism, and doomed to gradual if certain extinction. But they both agreed in desiring to conceal from their community all premature opening into the regions lighted by the sun; both were humane, and shrunk from the thought of annihilating so many millions of creatures; and the pictures I drew of our life, highly coloured as they were, saddened them. In

vain I boasted of our great men — poets, philosophers, orators, generals—and defied the Vril-ya
to produce their equals. "Alas!" said Zee, her
grand face softening into an angel-like compassion,
"this predominance of the few over the many is
the surest and most fatal sign of a race incorrigibly
savage. See you not that the primary condition of
mortal happiness consists in the extinction of that
strife and competition between individuals, which,
no matter what forms of government they adopt,
render the many subordinate to the few, destroy
real liberty to the individual, whatever may be the
nominal liberty of the state, and annul that calm
of existence, without which, felicity, mental or
bodily, cannot be attained? Our notion is, that
the more we can assimilate life to the existence
which our noblest ideas can conceive to be that
of spirits on the other side of the grave, why, the
more we approximate to a divine happiness here,
and the more easily we glide into the conditions
of being hereafter. For, surely, all we can imagine
of the life of gods, or of blessed immortals, sup-
poses the absence of self-made cares and con-

tentious passions, such as avarice and ambition.
It seems to us that it must be a life of serene
tranquillity, not indeed without active occupations
to the intellectual or spiritual powers, but occupations, of whatsoever nature they be, congenial to
the idiosyncrasies of each, not forced and repugnant
—a life gladdened by the untrammelled interchange of gentle affections, in which the moral
atmosphere utterly kills hate and vengeance, and
strife and rivalry. Such is the political state to
which all the tribes and families of the Vril-ya
seek to attain, and towards that goal all our theories
of government are shaped. You see how utterly
opposed is such a progress to that of the uncivilised
nations from which you come, and which aim at a
systematic perpetuity of troubles, and cares, and
warring passions, aggravated more and more as
their progress storms its way onward. The most
powerful of all the races in our world, beyond the
pale of the Vril-ya, esteems itself the best governed
of all political societies, and to have reached in
that respect the extreme end at which political
wisdom can arrive, so that the other nations should

tend more or less to copy it. It has established, on its broadest base, the Koom-Posh—viz., the government of the ignorant upon the principle of being the most numerous. It has placed the supreme bliss in the vying with each other in all things, so that the evil passions are never in repose—vying for power, for wealth, for eminence of some kind; and in this rivalry it is horrible to hear the vituperation, the slanders, and calumnies which even the best and mildest among them heap on each other without remorse or shame."

"Some years ago," said Aph-Lin, "I visited this people, and their misery and degradation were the more appalling because they were always boasting of their felicity and grandeur as compared with the rest of their species. And there is no hope that this people, which evidently resembles your own, can improve, because all their notions tend to further deterioration. They desire to enlarge their dominion more and more, in direct antagonism to the truth that, beyond a very limited range, it is impossible to secure to a community the happiness which belongs to a well-ordered family; and the

more they mature a system by which a few individuals are heated and swollen to a size above
the standard slenderness of the millions, the more
they chuckle and exact, and cry out, 'See by what
great exceptions to the common littleness of our
race we prove the magnificent results of our system!'"

"In fact," resumed Zee, "if the wisdom of human life be to approximate to the serene equality
of immortals, there can be no more direct flying off
into the opposite direction than a system which
aims at carrying to the utmost the inequalities and
turbulences of mortals. Nor do I see how, by any
forms of religious belief, mortals, so acting, could
fit themselves even to appreciate the joys of immortals to which they still expect to be transferred
by the mere act of dying. On the contrary, minds
accustomed to place happiness in things so much
the reverse of godlike, would find the happiness
of gods exceedingly dull, and would long to get
back to a world in which they could quarrel with
each other."

I HAVE spoken so much of the Vril Staff that my reader may expect me to describe it. This I cannot do accurately, for I was never allowed to handle it for fear of some terrible accident occasioned by my ignorance of its use. It is hollow, and has in the handle several stops, keys, or springs by which its force can be altered, modified, or directed—so that by one process it destroys, by another it heals—by one it can rend the rock, by another disperse the vapour—by one it affects bodies, by another it can exercise a certain influence over minds. It is usually carried in the convenient size of a walking-staff, but it has slides by which it can be lengthened or shortened at will. When used for special purposes, the upper part rests in the hollow of the palm with the fore and middle fingers protruded. I was assured, however, that its power was not equal in all, but proportioned

9*

to the amount of certain vril properties in the
wearer, in affinity, or *rapport*, with the purposes to
be effected. Some were more potent to destroy,
others to heal, &c.; much also depended on the
calm and steadiness of volition in the manipulator.
They assert that the full exercise of vril power can
only be acquired by constitutional temperament—
i. e., by hereditarily transmitted organisation—and
that a female infant of four years old belonging to
the Vril-ya races can accomplish feats with the
wand placed for the first time in her hand, which a
life spent in its practice would not enable the
strongest and most skilled mechanician, born out of
the pale of the Vril-ya, to achieve. All these wands
are not equally complicated; those intrusted to
children are much simpler than those borne by
sages of either sex, and constructed with a view to
the special object in which the children are employed; which, as I have before said, is among the
youngest children the most destructive. In the
wands of wives and mothers the correlative destroying force is usually abstracted, the healing power
fully charged. I wish I could say more in detail of

this singular conductor of the vril fluid, but its machinery is as exquisite as its effects are marvellous.

I should say, however, that this people have invented certain tubes by which the vril fluid can be
conducted towards the object it is meant to destroy,
throughout a distance almost indefinite; at least I
put it modestly when I say from 500 to 600 miles.
And their mathematical science as applied to such
purpose is so nicely accurate, that on the report of
some observer in an air-boat, any member of the
vril department can estimate unerringly the nature
of intervening obstacles, the height to which the
projectile instrument should be raised, and the extent to which it should be charged, so as to reduce
to ashes within a space of time too short for me to
venture to specify it, a capital twice as vast as
London.

Certainly these Ana are wonderful mechanicians
—wonderful for the adaptation of the inventive
faculty to practical uses.

I went with my host and his daughter Zee over
the great public museum, which occupies a wing in
the College of Sages, and in which are hoarded, as

curious specimens of the ignorant and blundering
experiments of ancient times, many contrivances on
which we pride ourselves as recent achievements.
In one department, carelessly thrown aside as obsolete lumber, are tubes for destroying life by metallic balls and an inflammable powder, on the principle of our cannons and catapults, and even still
more murderous than our latest improvements.

My host spoke of these with a smile of contempt, such as an artillery officer might bestow on
the bows and arrows of the Chinese. In another
department there were models of vehicles and ves-
sels worked by steam, and of a balloon which might
have been constructed by Montgolfier. "Such,"
said Zee, with an air of meditative wisdom—"such
were the feeble triflings with nature of our savage
forefathers, ere they had even a glimmering perception of the properties of vril!"

This young Gy was a magnificent specimen of
the muscular force to which the females of her
country attain. Her features were beautiful, like
those of all her race: never in the upper world
have I seen a face so grand and so faultless, but

her devotion to the severer studies had given to her countenance an expression of abstract thought which rendered it somewhat stern when in repose; and such sternness became formidable when observed in connection with her ample shoulders and lofty stature. She was tall even for a Gy, and I saw her lift up a cannon as easily as I could lift a pocket-pistol. Zee inspired me with a profound terror—a terror which increased when we came into a department of the museum appropriated to models of contrivances worked by the agency of vril; for here, merely by a certain play of her vril staff, she herself standing at a distance, she put into movement large and weighty substances. She seemed to endow them with intelligence, and to make them comprehend and obey her command. She set complicated pieces of machinery into movement, arrested the movement or continued it, until, within an incredibly short time, various kinds of raw material were reproduced as symmetrical works of art, complete and perfect. Whatever effect mesmerism or electro-biology produces over the nerves and muscles of animated objects, this young Gy pro-

duced by the motions of her slender rod over the
springs and wheels of lifeless mechanism.

When I mentioned to my companions my as-
tonishment at this influence over inanimate matter
—while owning that, in our world, I had witnessed
phenomena which showed that over certain living
organisations certain other living organisations
could establish an influence genuine in itself, but
often exaggerated by credulity or craft—Zee, who
was more interested in such subjects than her
father, bade me stretch forth my hand, and then
placing her own beside it, she called my attention
to certain distinctions of type and character. In the
first place, the thumb of the Gy (and, as I afterwards noticed, of all that race, male or female) was
much larger, at once longer and more massive, than
is found with our species above ground.   There is
almost, in this, as great a difference as there is between the thumb of a man and that of a gorilla.
Secondly, the palm is proportionately thicker than
ours—the texture of the skin infinitely finer and
softer—its average warmth is greater. More remarkable than all this, is a visible nerve, perceptible

under the skin, which starts from the wrist skirting
the ball of the thumb, and branching, fork-like, at
the roots of the fore and middle fingers. "With
your slight formation of thumb," said the philosophical young Gy, "and with the absence of the
nerve which you find more or less developed in the
hands of our race, you can never achieve other
than imperfect and feeble power over the agency of
vril; but so far as the nerve is concerned, that is
not found in the hands of our earliest progenitors,
nor in those of the ruder tribes without the pale of
the Vril-ya. It has been slowly developed in the
course of generations, commencing in the early
achievements, and increasing with the continuous
exercise, of the vril power; therefore, in the course
of one or two thousand years, such a nerve may
possibly be engendered in those higher beings of
your race, who devote themselves to that para-
mount science through which is attained command
over all the subtler forces of nature permeated by
vril. But when you talk of matter as something in
itself inert and motionless, your parents or tutors
surely cannot have left you so ignorant as not to

know that no form of matter is motionless and
inert: every particle is constantly in motion and
constantly acted upon by agencies, of which heat is
the most apparent and rapid, but vril the most
subtle, and, when skilfully wielded, the most powerful. So that, in fact, the current launched by my
hand and guided by my will does but render
quicker and more potent the action which is eter-
nally at work upon every particle of matter, however inert and stubborn it may seem. If a heap of
metal be not capable of originating a thought of its
own, yet, through its internal susceptibility to movement, it obtains the power to receive the thought
of the intellectual agent at work on it; and which,
when conveyed with a sufficient force of the vril
power, it is as much compelled to obey as if it were
displaced by a visible bodily force. It is animated
for the time being by the soul thus infused into it,
so that one may almost say that it lives and it reasons. Without this we could not make our automata
supply the place of servants."

I was too much in awe of the thews and the
learning of the young Gy to hazard the risk of

arguing with her. I had read somewhere in my schoolboy days that a wise man, disputing with a Roman emperor, suddenly drew in his horns; and when the emperor asked him whether he had nothing further to say on his side of the question, replied, "Nay, Cæsar, there is no arguing against a reasoner who commands twenty-five legions."

Though I had a secret persuasion that, whatever the real effects of vril upon matter, Mr. Faraday could have proved her a very shallow philosopher as to its extent or its causes, I had no doubt that Zee could have brained all the Fellows of the Royal Society, one after the other, with a blow of her fist. Every sensible man knows that it is useless to argue with any ordinary female upon matters he comprehends; but to argue with a Gy seven feet high upon the mysteries of vril,—as well argue in a desert, and with a simoom!

Amid the various departments to which the vast building of the College of Sages was appropriated, that which interested me most was devoted to the archæology of the Vril-ya, and comprised a very ancient collection of portraits. In these the pig-

ments and groundwork employed were of so durable
a nature that even pictures said to be executed at
dates as remote as those in the earliest annals of
the Chinese, retained much freshness of colour. In
examining this collection, two things especially
struck me:—firstly, That the pictures said to be between 6000 and 7000 years old were of a much
higher degree of art than any produced within the
last 3000 or 4000 years; and, secondly, That the
portraits within the former period much more resembled our own upper world and European types
of countenance. Some of them, indeed, reminded
me of the Italian heads which look out from the
canvas of Titian—speaking of ambition or craft, of
care or of grief, with furrows in which the passions
have passed with iron ploughshare. These were
the countenances of men who had lived in struggle
and conflict before the discovery of the latent forces
of vril had changed the character of society—men
who had fought with each other for power or fame
as we in the upper world fight.

'The type of face began to evince a marked
change about a thousand years after the vril revolu-

tion, becoming then, with each generation, more
serene, and in that serenity more terribly distinct
from the faces of labouring and sinful men; while
in proportion as the beauty and the grandeur of
the countenance itself became more fully developed,
the art of the painter became more tame and monotonous.

But the greatest curiosity in the collection was
that of three portraits belonging to the pre-historical
age, and, according to mythical tradition, taken by
the orders of a philosopher, whose origin and attributes were as much mixed up with symbolical
fable as those of an Indian Budh or a Greek Pro-
metheus.

From this mysterious personage, at once a sage
and a hero, all the principal sections of the Vril-ya
race pretend to trace a common origin.

The portraits are of the philosopher himself, of
his grandfather, and great-grandfather. They are
all at full length. The philosopher is attired in a
long tunic which seems to form a loose suit of
scaly armour, borrowed, perhaps, from some fish
or reptile, but the feet and hands are exposed: the

digits in both are wonderfully long, and webbed.
He has little or no perceptible throat, and a low
receding forehead, not at all the ideal of a sage's.
He has bright brown prominent eyes, a very wide
mouth and high cheek-bones, and a muddy complexion. According to tradition, this philosopher
had lived to a patriarchal age, extending over many
centuries, and he remembered distinctly in middle
life his grandfather as surviving, and in childhood
his great-grandfather; the portrait of the first he had
taken, or caused to be taken, while yet alive—that
of the latter was taken from his effigies in mummy.
The portrait of the grandfather had the features
and aspect of the philosopher, only much more exaggerated: he was not dressed, and the colour of
his body was singular; the breast and stomach
yellow, the shoulders and legs of a dull bronze
hue: the great-grandfather was a magnificent specimen
of the Batrachian genus, a Giant Frog, *pur et
simple*.

Among the pithy sayings which, according to
tradition, the philosopher bequeathed to posterity
in rhythmical form and sententious brevity, this is

notably recorded: "Humble yourselves, my descendants; the father of your race was a *tnad* (tadpole): exalt yourselves, my descendants, for it was
the same Divine Thought which created your father
that develops itself in exalting you."

Aph-Lin told me this fable while I gazed on
the three Batrachian portraits. I said in reply:
"You make a jest of my supposed ignorance and
credulity as an uneducated Tish, but though these
horrible daubs may be of great antiquity, and were
intended, perhaps, for some rude caricature, I presume that none of your race, even in the less enlightened ages, ever believed that the great-grandson
of a Frog became a sententious philosopher; or
that any section, I will not say of the lofty Vril-ya,
but of the meanest varieties of the human race,
had its origin in a Tadpole."

"Pardon me," answered Aph-Lin: "in what we
call the Wrangling or Philosophical Period of
History, which was at its height about seven thousand years ago, there was a very distinguished naturalist, who proved to the satisfaction of numerous
disciples such analogical and anatomical agreements

in structure between an An and a Frog, as to show
that out of the one must have developed the other.
They had some diseases in common; they were
both subject to the same parasitical worms in the
intestines; and, strange to say, the An has, in his
structure, a swimming-bladder, no longer of any
use to him, but which is a rudiment that clearly
proves his descent from a Frog. Nor is there any
argument against this theory to be found in the
relative difference of size, for there are still existent
in our world Frogs of a size and stature not inferior to our own, and many thousand years ago
they appear to have been still larger."

"I understand that," said I, "because Frogs thus
enormous are, according to our eminent geologists,
who perhaps saw them in dreams, said to have been
distinguished inhabitants of the upper world before
the Deluge; and such Frogs are exactly the creatures likely to have flourished in the lakes and
morasses of your subterranean regions. But pray,
proceed."

"In the Wrangling Period of History, whatever
one sage asserted another sage was sure to contra-

dict. In fact, it was a maxim in that age, that the
human reason could only be sustained aloft by
being tossed to and fro in the perpetual motion of
contradiction; and therefore another sect of philosophers maintained the doctrine that the An was
not the descendant of the Frog, but that the Frog
was clearly the improved development of the An.
The shape of the Frog, taken generally, was much
more symmetrical than that of the An; beside the
beautiful conformation of its lower limbs, its flanks
and shoulders, the majority of the Ana in that day
were almost deformed, and certainly ill-shaped.
Again, the Frog had the power to live alike on
land and in water—a mighty privilege, partaking
of a spiritual essence denied to the An, since the
disuse of his swimming-bladder clearly proves his
degeneration from a higher development of species.
Again, the earlier races of the Ana seem to have
been covered with hair, and, even to a comparatively recent date, hirsute bushes deformed the
very faces of our ancestors, spreading wild over
their cheeks and chins, as similar bushes, my poor
Tish, spread wild over yours. But the object of

the higher races of the Ana through countless generations has been to erase all vestige of connection
with hairy vertebrata, and they have gradually eli-
minated that debasing capillary excrement by the
law of sexual selection; the Gy-ei naturally pre-
ferring youth or the beauty of smooth faces. But
the degree of the Frog in the scale of the vertebrata
is shown in this, that he has no hair at all, not even
on his head. He was born to that hairless perfection which the most beautiful of the Ana, despite
the culture of incalculable ages, have not yet attained. The wonderful complication and delicacy
of a Frog's nervous system and arterial circulation
were shown by this school to be more susceptible
of enjoyment than our inferior, or at least simpler,
physical frame allows us to be. The examination
of a Frog's hand, if I may use that expression, ac-
counted for its keener susceptibility to love, and to
social life in general. In fact, gregarious and ama-
tory as are the Ana, Frogs are still more so. In
short, these two schools raged against each other;
one asserting the An to be the perfected type of
the Frog; the other that the Frog was the highest

development of the An. The moralists were divided
in opinion with the naturalists, but the bulk of them
sided with the Frog-preference school. They said,
with much plausibility, that in moral conduct (viz.,
in the adherence to rules best adapted to the health
and welfare of the individual and the community)
there could be no doubt of the vast superiority of
the Frog. All history showed the wholesale im-
morality of the human race, the complete disregard,
even by the most renowned among them, of the
laws which they acknowledged to be essential to
their own and the general happiness and wellbeing.
But the severest critic of the Frog race could not
detect in their manners a single aberration from the
moral law tacitly recognised by themselves. And
what, after all, can be the profit of civilisation if
superiority in moral conduct be not the aim for
which it strives, and the test by which its progress
should be judged?

"In fine, the adherents to this theory presumed
that in some remote period the Frog race had been
the improved development of the Human; but that,
from causes which defied rational conjecture, they

10*

had not maintained their original position in the
scale of nature; while the Ana, though of inferior
organisation, had, by dint less of their virtues than
their vices, such as ferocity and cunning, gradually
acquired ascendancy, much as among the human
race itself tribes utterly barbarous have, by superiority in similar vices, utterly destroyed or reduced
into insignificance tribes originally excelling them
in mental gifts and culture.   Unhappily these disputes became involved with the religious notions of
that age; and as society was then administered
under the government of the Koom-Posh, who,
being the most ignorant, were of course the most
inflammable class—the multitude took the whole
question out of the hands of the philosophers; political chiefs saw that the Frog dispute, so taken up
by the populace, could become a most valuable instrument of their ambition; and for not less than
one thousand years war and massacre prevailed,
during which period the philosophers on both sides
were butchered, and the government of the Koom-
Posh itself was happily brought to an end by the
ascendancy of a family that clearly established its

descent from the aboriginal tadpole, and furnished despotic rulers to the various nations of the Ana. These despots finally disappeared, at least from our communities, as the discovery of vril led to the tranquil institutions under which flourish all the races of the Vril-ya."

"And do no wranglers or philosophers now exist to revive the dispute; or do they all recognise the origin of your race in the tadpole?"

"Nay, such disputes," said Zee, with a lofty smile, "belong to the Pah-bodh of the dark ages, and now only serve for the amusement of infants. When we know the elements out of which our bodies are composed, elements common to the humblest vegetable plants, can it signify whether the All-Wise combined those elements out of one form more than another, in order to create that in which He has placed the capacity to receive the idea of Himself, and all the varied grandeurs of intellect to which that idea gives birth? The An in reality commenced to exist as An with the donation of that capacity, and, with that capacity, the sense to acknowledge that, however through the countless ages his race may improve in wisdom, it can never combine the elements at its command into the form of a tadpole."

"You speak well, Zee," said Aph-Lin; "and it is enough for us shortlived mortals to feel a reasonable assurance that whether the origin of the An was a tadpole or not, he is no more likely to become a tadpole again than the institutions of the Vril-ya are likely to relapse into the heaving quagmire and certain strife-rot of a Koom-Posh."

CHAPTER XVII.

THE Vril-ya, being excluded from all sight of
the heavenly bodies, and having no other difference
between night and day than that which they deem
it convenient to make for themselves,—do not, of
course, arrive at their divisions of time by the same
process that we do; but I found it easy, by the aid
of my watch, which I luckily had about me, to
compute their time with great nicety. I reserve
for a future work on the science and literature of
the Vril-ya, should I live to complete it, all details
as to the manner in which they arrive at their no-
tation of time; and content myself here with saying,
that in point of duration, their year differs very
slightly from ours, but that the divisions of their
year are by no means the same. Their day (including what we call night) consists of twenty hours
of our time, instead of twenty-four, and of course
their year comprises the correspondent increase in
the number of days by which it is summed up.

They subdivide the twenty hours of their day thus
—eight hours,* called the "Silent Hours," for repose; eight hours, called the "Earnest Time," for
the pursuits and occupations of life; and four
hours, called the "Easy Time" (with which what I
may term their day closes), allotted to festivities,
sport, recreation, or family converse, according to
their several tastes and inclinations. But, in truth,
out of doors there is no night. They maintain,
both in the streets and in the surrounding country,
to the limits of their territory, the same degree of
light at all hours. Only, within doors, they lower
it to a soft twilight during the Silent Hours. They
have a great horror of perfect darkness, and their
lights are never wholly extinguished. On occasions
of festivity they continue the duration of full light,
but equally keep note of the distinction between
night and day, by mechanical contrivances which
answer the purpose of our clocks and watches.
They are very fond of music; and it is by music
that these chronometers strike the principal division

* For the sake of convenience, I adopt the words hours, days, years,
&c., in any general reference to subdivisions of time among the Vril-ya—
those terms but loosely corresponding, however, with such subdivisions.

of time. At every one of their hours, during their
day, the sounds coming from all the time-pieces in
their public buildings, and caught up, as it were,
by those of houses or hamlets scattered amidst the
landscapes without the city, have an effect singularly sweet, and yet singularly solemn. But during the Silent Hours these sounds are so subdued
as to be only faintly heard by a waking ear. They
have no change of seasons, and, at least in the territory of this tribe, the atmosphere seemed to me
very equable, warm as that of an Italian summer,
and humid rather than dry; in the forenoon usually
very still, but at times invaded by strong blasts
from the rocks that made the borders of their domain. But time is the same to them for sowing or
reaping as in the Golden Isles of the ancient poets.
At the same moment you see the younger plants in
blade or bud, the older in ear or fruit. All fruit-
bearing plants, however, after fruitage, either shed
or change the colour of their leaves. But that
which interested me most in reckoning up their
divisions of time was the ascertainment of the
average duration of life amongst them. I found on

minute inquiry that this very considerably exceeded
the term allotted to us on the upper earth. What
seventy years are to us, one hundred years are to
them. Nor is this the only advantage they have
over us in longevity, for as few among us attain to
the age of seventy, so, on the contrary, few among
them die before the age of one hundred; and they
enjoy a general degree of health and vigour which
makes life itself a blessing even to the last. Various
causes contribute to this result: the absence of all
alcoholic stimulants; temperance in food; more
especially, perhaps, a serenity of mind undisturbed
by anxious occupations and eager passions. They
are not tormented by our avarice or our ambition;
they appear perfectly indifferent even to the desire
of fame; they are capable of great affection, but
their love shows itself in a tender and cheerful
complaisance, and, while forming their happiness,
seems rarely, if ever, to constitute their woe. As
the Gy is sure only to marry where she herself
fixes her choice, and as here, not less than above
ground, it is the female on whom the happiness of
home depends; so the Gy, having chosen the mate

she prefers to all others, is lenient to his faults,
consults his humours, and does her best to secure
his attachment. The death of a beloved one is of
course with them, as with us, a cause of sorrow;
but not only is death with them so much more
rare before that age in which it becomes a release,
but when it does occur the survivor takes much
more consolation than, I am afraid, the generality
of us do, in the certainty of reunion in another
and yet happier life.

All these causes, then, concur to their healthful
and enjoyable longevity, though, no doubt, much
also must be owing to hereditary organisation. According to their records, however, in those earlier
stages of their society when they lived in communities resembling ours, agitated by fierce competition, their lives were considerably shorter, and
their maladies more numerous and grave. They
themselves say that the duration of life, too, has
increased, and is still on the increase, since their
discovery of the invigorating and medicinal properties of vril, applied for remedial purposes. They
have few professional and regular practitioners of

medicine, and these are chiefly Gy·ei, who, especially if widowed and childless, find great delight in the healing art, and even undertake surgical operations in those cases required by accident, or, more rarely, by disease.

They have their diversions and entertainments, and, during the Easy Time of their day, they are wont to assemble in great numbers for those winged sports in the air which I have already described. They have also public halls for music, and even theatres, at which are performed pieces that appeared to me somewhat to resemble the plays of the Chinese—dramas that are thrown back into distant times for their events and personages, in which all classic unities are outrageously violated, and the hero, in one scene a child, in the next is an old man, and so forth. These plays are of very ancient composition. They appeared to me extremely dull, on the whole, but were relieved by startling mechanical contrivances, and a kind of farcical broad humour, and detached passages of great vigour and power expressed in language highly poetical, but somewhat overcharged with metaphor and trope. In fine, they seemed to me very much what the plays of Shakespeare seemed to a Parisian in the time of Louis XV., or perhaps to an Englishman in the reign of Charles II.

The audience, of which the Gy-ei constituted the chief portion, appeared to enjoy greatly the representation of these dramas, which, for so sedate and majestic a race of females, surprised me, till I observed that all the performers were under the age of adolescence, and conjectured truly that the mothers and sisters came to please their children and brothers.

I have said that these dramas are of great antiquity. No new plays, indeed no imaginative works sufficiently important to survive their immediate day, appear to have been composed for several generations. In fact, though there is no lack of new publications, and they have even what may be called newspapers, these are chiefly devoted to mechanical science, reports of new inventions, announcements respecting various details of business—in short, to practical matters. Sometimes a child writes a little tale of adventure, or a young

Gy vents her amorous hopes or fears in a poem;
but these effusions are of very little merit, and are
seldom read except by children and maiden Gy-ei.
The most interesting works of a purely literary
character are those of explorations and travels into
other regions of this nether world, which are generally written by young emigrants, and are read with
great avidity by the relations and friends they have
left behind.

I could not help expressing to Aph-Lin my surprise that a community in which mechanical science
had made so marvellous a progress, and in which
intellectual civilisation had exhibited itself in realising those objects for the happiness of the people,
which the political philosophers above ground had,
after ages of struggle, pretty generally agreed to
consider unattainable visions, should, nevertheless,
be so wholly without a contemporaneous literature,
despite the excellence to which culture had brought
a language at once rich and simple, vigorous and
musical.

My host replied—"Do you not perceive that a
literature such as you mean would be wholly in-

compatible with that perfection of social or political
felicity at which you do us the honour to think we
have arrived? We have at last, after centuries of
struggle, settled into a form of government with
which we are content, and in which, as we allow
no differences of rank, and no honours are paid to
administrators distinguishing them from others, there
is no stimulus given to individual ambition. No
one would read works advocating theories that involved any political or social change, and therefore
no one writes them. If now and then an An feels
himself dissatisfied with our tranquil mode of life,
he does not attack it; he goes away. Thus all that
part of literature (and to judge by the ancient
books in our public libraries, it was once a very
large part) which relates to speculative theories on
society is become utterly extinct. Again, formerly
there was a vast deal written respecting the attributes and essence of the All-Good, and the
arguments for and against a future state; but now
we all recognise two facts, that there *is* a Divine
Being, and there *is* a future state, and we all
equally agree that if we wrote our fingers to the

bone, we could not throw any light upon the nature and conditions of that future state, or quicken our apprehensions of the attributes and essence of that Divine Being. Thus another part of literature has become also extinct, happily for our race; for in the times when so much was written on subjects which no one could determine, people seemed to live in a perpetual state of quarrel and contention. So, too, a vast part of our ancient literature consists of historical records of wars and revolutions during the times when the Ana lived in large and turbulent societies, each seeking aggrandisement at the expense of the other. You see our serene mode of life now; such it has been for ages. We have no events to chronicle. What more of us can be said than that 'they were born, they were happy, they died!' Coming next to that part of literature which is more under the control of the imagination, such as what we call Glaubsila, or colloquially 'Glaubs,' and you call poetry, the reasons for its decline amongst us are abundantly obvious.

"We find, by referring to the great masterpieces in that department of literature which we all still read with pleasure, but of which none would tolerate imitations, that they consist in the portraiture of passions which we no longer experience—ambition, vengeance, unhallowed love, the thirst for warlike renown, and suchlike. The old poets lived in an atmosphere impregnated with these passions, and felt vividly what they expressed glowingly. No one can express such passions now, for no one can feel them, or meet with any sympathy in his readers if he did. Again, the old poetry has a main element in its dissection of those complex mysteries of human character which conduce to abnormal vices and crimes, or lead to signal and extraordinary virtues. But our society, having got rid of temptations to any prominent vices and crimes, has necessarily rendered the moral average so equal, that there are no very salient virtues. Without its ancient food of strong passions, vast crimes, heroic excellences, poetry therefore is, if not actually starved to death, reduced to a very meagre diet. There is still the poetry of description—description of rocks, and trees, and waters, and common household life; and our young Gy-ei weave much of

this insipid kind of composition into their love
verses."

"Such poetry," said I, "might surely be made
very charming; and we have critics amongst us
who consider it a higher kind than that which
depicts the crimes, or analyses the passions, of man.
At all events, poetry of the insipid kind you mention is a poetry that nowadays commands more
readers than any other among the people I have
left above ground."

"Possibly; but then I suppose the writers take
great pains with the language they employ, and
devote themselves to the culture and polish of
words and rhythms as an art?"

"Certainly they do: all great poets must do
that. Though the gift of poetry may be inborn, the
gift requires as much care to make it available as
a block of metal does to be made into one of your
engines."

"And doubtless your poets have some incen-
tive to bestow all those pains upon such verbal
prettinesses?"

"Well, I presume their instinct of song would

make them sing as the bird does; but to cultivate the song into verbal or artificial prettiness, probably does need an inducement from without, and our poets find it in the love of fame—perhaps, now and then, in the want of money."

"Precisely so But in our society we attach fame to nothing which man, in that moment of his duration which is called 'life,' can perform. We should soon lose that equality which constitutes the felicitous essence of our commonwealth if we selected any individual for pre-eminent praise: pre-eminent praise would confer pre-eminent power, and the moment it were given, evil passions, now dormant, would awake; other men would immediately covet praise, then would arise envy, and with envy hate, and with hate calumny and persecution. Our history tells us that most of the poets and most of the writers who, in the old time, were favoured with the greatest praise, were also assailed by the greatest vituperation, and even, on the whole, rendered very unhappy, partly by the attacks of jealous rivals, partly by the diseased mental constitution which an acquired sensitiveness to praise and to blame tends

11*

to engender. As for the stimulus of want; in the
first place, no man in our community knows the
goad of poverty; and, secondly, if he did, almost
every occupation would be more lucrative than
writing.

"Our public libraries contain all the books of
the past which time has preserved; those books, for
the reasons above stated, are infinitely better than
any can write nowadays, and they are open to all
to read without cost. We are not such fools as to
pay for reading inferior books, when we can read
superior books for nothing."

"With us, novelty has an attraction; and a new
book, if bad, is read when an old book, though
good, is neglected."

"Novelty, to barbarous states of society strug-
gling in despair for something better, has no doubt
an attraction, denied to us, who see nothing to gain
in novelties; but, after all, it is observed by one of
our great authors four thousand years ago, that 'he
who studies old books will always find in them
something new, and he who reads new books will
always find in them something old.' But to return

to the question you have raised, there being then among us no stimulus to painstaking labour, whether in desire of fame or in pressure of want, such as have the poetic temperament, no doubt, vent it in song, as you say the bird sings; but for lack of elaborate culture it fails of an audience, and, failing of an audience, dies out, of itself, amidst the ordinary avocations of life."

"But how is it that these discouragements to the cultivation of literature do not operate against that of science?"

"Your question amazes me. The motive to science is the love of truth apart from all consideration of fame, and science with us too is devoted almost solely to practical uses, essential to our social conservation and the comforts of our daily life. No fame is asked by the inventor, and none is given to him; he enjoys an occupation congenial to his tastes, and needing no wear and tear of the passions. Man must have exercise for his mind as well as body; and continuous exercise, rather than violent, is best for both. Our most ingenious cultivators of science are, as a general rule, the longest

lived and the most free from disease. Painting is
an amusement to many, but the art is not what it
was in former times, when the great painters in our
various communities vied with each other for the
prize of a golden crown, which gave them a social
rank equal to that of the kings under whom they
lived. You will thus doubtless have observed in
our archæological department how superior in point
of art the pictures were several thousand years ago.
Perhaps it is because music is, in reality, more allied
to science than it is to poetry, that, of all the
pleasurable arts, music is that which flourishes the
most amongst us. Still, even in music the absence
of stimulus in praise or fame has served to prevent
any great superiority of one individual over another;
and we rather excel in choral music, with the aid
of our vast mechanical instruments, in which we
make great use of the agency of water,* than in
single performers. We have had scarcely any
original composer for some ages. Our favourite

* This may remind the student of Nero's invention of a musical
machine, by which water was made to perform the part of an orchestra,
and on which he was employed when the conspiracy against him broke
out.

airs are very ancient in substance, but have admitted many complicated variations by inferior, though ingenious, musicians."

"Are there no political societies among the Ana which are animated by those passions, subjected to those crimes, and admitting those disparities in condition, in intellect, and in morality, which the state of your tribe, or indeed of the Vril-ya generally, has left behind in its progress to perfection? If so, among such societies perhaps Poetry and her sister arts still continue to be honoured and to improve?"

"There are such societies in remote regions, but we do not admit them within the pale of civilised communities; we scarcely even give them the name of Ana, and certainly not that of Vril-ya. They are barbarians, living chiefly in that low stage of being, Koom-Posh, tending necessarily to its own hideous dissolution in Glek-Nas. Their wretched existence is passed in perpetual contest and perpetual change. When they do not fight with their neighbours, they fight among themselves. They are divided into sections, which abuse, plunder, and sometimes murder each other, and on the most frivolous points of difference that would be unintelligible to us if we had not read history, and seen that we too have passed through the same early state of ignorance and barbarism. Any trifle is sufficient to set them together by the ears. They pretend to be all equals, and the more they have struggled to be so, by removing old distinctions and starting afresh, the more glaring and intolerable the disparity becomes, because nothing in hereditary affections and associations is left to soften the one naked distinction between the many who have nothing and the few who have much. Of course the many hate the few, but without the few they could not live. The many are always assailing the few; sometimes they exterminate the few; but as soon as they have done so, a new few starts out of the many, and is harder to deal with than the old few. For where societies are large, and competition to have something is the predominant fever, there must be always many losers and few gainers. In short, the people I speak of are savages groping their way in the dark towards some gleam of light, and would demand

our commiseration for their infirmities, if, like all
savages, they did not provoke their own destruction
by their arrogance and cruelty. Can you imagine that
creatures of this kind, armed only with such miser-
able weapons as you may see in our museum of
antiquities, clumsy iron tubes charged with saltpetre,
have more than once threatened with destruction a
tribe of the Vril-ya, which dwells nearest to them,
because they say they have thirty millions of population—and that tribe may have fifty thousand—if
the latter do not accept their notions of Soc-Sec
(money-getting) on some trading principles which
they have the impudence to call a 'law of civilisation!'"

"But thirty millions of population are formidable
odds against fifty thousand!"

My host stared at me astonished. "Stranger,"
said he, "you could not have heard me say that
this threatened tribe belongs to the Vril-ya; and it
only waits for these savages to declare war, in order
to commission some half-a-dozen small children to
sweep away their whole population."

At these words I felt a thrill of horror, recog-

nising much more affinity with "the savages" than
I did with the Vril-ya, and remembering all I had
said in praise of the glorious American institutions,
which Aph-Lin stigmatised as Koom-Posh. Recovering my self-possession, I asked if there were
modes of transit by which I could safely visit this
temerarious and remote people.

"You can travel with safety, by vril agency,
either along the ground or amid the air, throughout
all the range of the communities with which we are
allied and akin; but I cannot vouch for your safety
in barbarous nations governed by different laws
from ours; nations, indeed, so benighted, that there
are among them large numbers who actually live by
stealing from each other, and one could not with
safety in the Silent Hours even leave the doors of
one's own house open."

Here our conversation was interrupted by the
entrance of Taë, who came to inform us that he,
having been deputed to discover and destroy the
enormous reptile which I had seen on my first ar-
rival, had been on the watch for it ever since his
visit to me, and had begun to suspect that my eyes

had deceived me, or that the creature had made its
way through the cavities within the rocks to the
wild regions in which dwelt its kindred race,—
when it gave evidences of its whereabouts by a
great devastation of the herbage bordering one of
the lakes. "And," said Taë, "I feel sure that within
that lake it is now hiding. So" (turning to me) "I
thought it might amuse you to accompany me to
see the way we destroy such unpleasant visitors."
As I looked at the face of the young child, and
called to mind the enormous size of the creature
he proposed to exterminate, I felt myself shudder
with fear for him, and perhaps fear for myself, if I
accompanied him in such a chase. But my curiosity
to witness the destructive effects of the boasted vril,
and my unwillingness to lower myself in the eyes
of an infant by betraying apprehensions of personal
safety, prevailed over my first impulse. Accord-
ingly, I thanked Taë for his courteous consideration
for my amusement, and professed my willingness to
set out with him on so diverting an enterprise.

CHAPTER XVIII.

As Taë and myself, on quitting the town, and leaving to the left the main road which led to it, struck into the fields, the strange and solemn beauty of the landscape, lighted up, by numberless lamps, to the verge of the horizon, fascinated my eyes, and rendered me for some time an inattentive listener to the talk of my companion.

Along our way various operations of agriculture were being carried on by machinery, the forms of which were new to me, and for the most part very graceful; for among these people art being so cultivated for the sake of mere utility, exhibits itself in adorning or refining the shapes of useful objects. Precious metals and gems are so profuse among them, that they are lavished on things devoted to purposes the most commonplace; and their love of utility leads them to beautify its tools, and quickens their imagination in a way unknown to themselves.

In all service, whether in or out of doors, they make great use of automaton figures, which are so ingenious, and so pliant to the operations of vril, that they actually seem gifted with reason. It was scarcely possible to distinguish the figures I beheld, apparently guiding or superintending the rapid movements of vast engines, from human forms endowed with thought.

By degrees, as we continued to walk on, my attention became roused by the lively and acute remarks of my companion. The intelligence of the children among this race is marvellously precocious, perhaps from the habit of having intrusted to them, at so early an age, the toils and responsibilities of middle age. Indeed, in conversing with Taë, I felt as if talking with some superior and observant man of my own years. I asked him if he could form any estimate of the number of communities into which the race of the Vril-ya is subdivided.

"Not exactly," he said, "because they multiply, of course, every year as the surplus of each community is drafted off. But I heard my father say that, according to the last report, there were a mil-

lion and a half of communities speaking our language, and adopting our institutions and forms of
life and government; but, I believe, with some differences, about which you had better ask Zee. She
knows more than most of the Ana do. An An cares
less for things that do not concern him than a Gy
does; the Gy-ei are inquisitive creatures."

"Does each community restrict itself to the
same number of families or amount of population
that you do?"

"No; some have much smaller populations,
some have larger—varying according to the extent
of the country they appropriate, or to the degree
of excellence to which they have brought their
machinery. Each community sets its own limit
according to circumstances, taking care always that
there shall never arise any class of poor by the
pressure of population upon the productive powers
of the domain; and that no state shall be too large
for a government resembling that of a single well-
ordered family. I imagine that no Vril community
exceeds thirty thousand households. But, as a
general rule, the smaller the community, provided

there be hands enough to do justice to the capacities
of the territory it occupies, the richer each individual is, and the larger the sum contributed to
the general treasury,—above all, the happier and
the more tranquil is the whole political body, and
the more perfect the products of its industry. The
state which all tribes of the Vril-ya acknowledge
to be the highest in civilisation, and which has
brought the vril force to its fullest development, is
perhaps the smallest. It limits itself to four thousand families; but every inch of its territory is
cultivated to the utmost perfection of garden
ground; its machinery excels that of every other
tribe, and there is no product of its industry in
any department which is not sought for, at extraordinary prices, by each community of our race.
All our tribes make this state their model, considering that we should reach the highest state of
civilisation allowed to mortals if we could unite the
greatest degree of happiness with the highest degree
of intellectual achievement; and it is clear that the
smaller the society the less difficult that will be.
Ours is too large for it."

This reply set me thinking. I reminded myself
of that little state of Athens, with only twenty thousand free citizens, and which to this day our
mightiest nations regard as the supreme guide and
model in all departments of intellect. But then
Athens permitted fierce rivalry and perpetual
change, and was certainly not happy. Rousing
myself from the reverie into which these reflections
had plunged me, I brought back our talk to the
subjects connected with emigration.

"But," said I, "when, I suppose yearly, a certain
number among you agree to quit home and found
a new community elsewhere, they must necessarily
be very few, and scarcely sufficient, even with the
help of the machines they take with them, to clear
the ground, and build towns, and form a civilised
state with the comforts and luxuries in which they
had been reared."

"You mistake. All the tribes of the Vril-ya
are in constant communication with each other,
and settle amongst themselves each year what
proportion of one community will unite with the
emigrants of another, so as to form a state of

sufficient size; and the place for emigration is
agreed upon at least a year before, and pioneers
sent from each state to level rocks, and embank
waters, and construct houses; so that when the
emigrants at last go, they find a city already made,
and a country around it at least partially cleared.
Our hardy life as children makes us take cheerfully
to travel and adventure. I mean to emigrate myself when of age."

"Do the emigrants always select places hitherto
uninhabited and barren?"

"As yet generally, because it is our rule never
to destroy except where necessary to our wellbeing. Of course, we cannot settle in lands already
occupied by the Vril-ya; and if we take the cultivated lands of the other races of Ana, we must
utterly destroy the previous inhabitants. Sometimes,
as it is, we take waste spots, and find that a trouble-
some, quarrelsome race of Ana, especially if under
the administration of Koom-Posh or Glek-Nas,
resents our vicinity, and picks a quarrel with us;
then, of course, as menacing our welfare, we
destroy it: there is no coming to terms of peace |

with a race so idiotic that it is always changing
the form of government which represents it.
Koom-Posh," said the child, emphatically, "is bad
enough, still it has brains, though at the back
of its head, and is not without a heart; but in
Glek-Nas the brain and heart of the creatures
disappear, and they become all jaws, claws, and
belly."

"You express yourself strongly. Allow me to
inform you that I myself, and I am proud to say
it, am the citizen of a Koom-Posh."

"I no longer," answered Taë, "wonder to see
you here so far from your home. What was the
condition of your native community before it became a Koom-Posh?"

"A settlement of emigrants—like those settlements which your tribe sends forth—but so far
unlike your settlements, that it was dependent on
the state from which it came. It shook off that
yoke, and, crowned with eternal glory, became a
Koom-Posh."

"Eternal glory! how long has the Koom-Posh
lasted?"

"About 100 years."

"The length of an An's life—a very young community. In much less than another 100 years your Koom-Posh will be a Glek-Nas."

"Nay, the oldest states in the world I come from, have such faith in its duration, that they are all gradually shaping their institutions so as to melt into ours, and their most thoughtful politicians say that, whether they like it or not, the inevitable tendency of these old states is towards Koom-Posherie."

"The old states!"

"Yes, the old states."

"With populations very small in proportion to the area of productive land!"

"On the contrary, with populations very large in proportion to that area."

"I see! old states indeed!—so old as to become drivelling if they don't pack off that surplus population as we do ours—very old states!—very, very old! Pray, Tish, do you think it wise for very old men to try to turn head-over-heels as very young children do! And if you asked them why

12*

they attempted such antics, should you not laugh
if they answered that by imitating very young children they could become very young children themselves? Ancient history abounds with instances of
this sort a great many thousand years ago—and in
every instance a very old state that played at
Koom-Posh soon tumbled into Glek-Nas. Then,
in horror of its own self, it cried out for a master,
as an old man in his dotage cries out for a nurse;
and after a succession of masters or nurses, more
or less long, that very old state died out of history.
A very old state attempting Koom-Posh-erie is like
a very old man who pulls down the house to which
he has been accustomed, but he has so exhausted
his vigour in pulling down, that all he can do in
the way of rebuilding is to run up a crazy hut, in
which himself and his successors whine out, 'How
the wind blows! How the walls shake!'"

"My dear Tae, I make all excuse for your
unenlightened prejudices, which every schoolboy
educated in a Koom-Posh could easily controvert,
though he might not be so precociously learned in
ancient history as you appear to be."

"I learned! not a bit of it. But would a schoolboy, educated in your Koom-Posh, ask his great-great-grandfather or great-great-grandmother to stand on his or her head with the feet uppermost! and if the poor old folks hesitated—say, 'What do you fear!—see how I do it!'"

"Tae, I disdain to argue with a child of your age. I repeat, I make allowances for your want of that culture which a Koom-Posh alone can bestow."

"I, in my turn," answered Tae, with an air of the suave but lofty good breeding which characterises his race, "not only make allowances for you as not educated among the Vril-ya, but I entreat you to vouchsafe me your pardon for insufficient respect to the habits and opinions of so amiable a—Tish!"

I ought before to have observed that I was commonly called Tish by my host and his family, as being a polite and indeed a pet name, metaphorically signifying a small barbarian, literally a Froglet; the children apply it endearingly to the

tame species of Frog which they keep in their
gardens.

We had now reached the banks of a lake, and
Taë here paused to point out to me the ravages
made in fields skirting it. "The enemy certainly
lies within these waters," said Taë. "Observe
what shoals of fish are crowded together at the
margin. Even the great fishes with the small ones,
who are their habitual prey and who generally
shun them, all forget their instincts in the presence
of a common destroyer. This reptile certainly
must belong to the class of Krek-a, a class more
devouring than any other, and said to be among
the few surviving species of the world's dreadest
inhabitants before the Ana were created. The
appetite of a Krek is insatiable—it feeds alike
upon vegetable and animal life; but for the swift-
footed creatures of the elk species it is too slow in
its movements. Its favourite dainty is an An when
it can catch him unawares; and hence the Ana
destroy it relentlessly whenever it enters their
dominion. I have heard that when our forefathers
first cleared this country, these monsters, and others

like them, abounded, and, vril being then un-
discovered, many of our race were devoured. It
was impossible to exterminate them wholly till that
discovery which constitutes the power and sustains
the civilisation of our race. But after the uses of
vril became familiar to us, all creatures inimical
to us were soon annihilated. Still, once a-year
or so, one of these enormous reptiles wanders
from the unreclaimed and savage districts beyond,
and within my memory one seized upon a young
Gy who was bathing in this very lake. Had she
been on land and armed with her staff, it would
not have dared even to show itself; for, like all
savage creatures, the reptile has a marvellous
instinct, which warns it against the bearer of the
vril wand. How they teach their young to avoid
him, though seen for the first time, is one of those
mysteries which you may ask Zee to explain, for I
cannot.* So long as I stand here, the monster
will not stir from its lurking-place; but we must
now decoy it forth."

* The reptile in this instinct does but resemble our wild birds and
animals, which will not come in reach of a man armed with a gun. When

"Will not that be difficult?"

"Not at all. Seat yourself yonder on that crag (about one hundred yards from the bank), while I retire to a distance. In a short time the reptile will catch sight or scent of you, and, perceiving that you are no vril-bearer, will come forth to devour you. As soon as it is fairly out of the water, it becomes my prey."

"Do you mean to tell me that I am to be the decoy to that horrible monster which could engulf me within its jaws in a second? I beg to decline."

The child laughed. "Fear nothing," said he; "only sit still."

Instead of obeying this command, I made a bound, and was about to take fairly to my heels, when Taë touched me lightly on the shoulder, and, fixing his eyes steadily on mine, I was rooted to the spot. All power of volition left me. Submissive to the infant's gesture, I followed him to the crag he had indicated, and seated myself there in

---

the electric wires were first put up, partridges struck against them in their flight, and fell down wounded. No younger generation of partridges meet with a similar accident.

silence. Most readers have seen something of the effects of electro-biology, whether genuine or spurious. No professor of that doubtful craft had ever been able to influence a thought or a movement of mine, but I was a mere machine at the will of this terrible child. Meanwhile he expanded his wings, soared aloft, and alighted amidst a copse at the brow of a hill at some distance.

I was alone; and turning my eyes with an indescribable sensation of horror towards the lake, I kept them fixed on its water, spell-bound. It might be ten or fifteen minutes, to me it seemed ages, before the still surface, gleaming under the lamp-light, began to be agitated towards the centre. At the same time the shoals of fish near the margin evinced their sense of the enemy's approach by splash and leap and bubbling circle. I could detect their hurried flight hither and thither, some even casting themselves ashore. A long, dark, undulous furrow came moving along the waters, nearer and nearer, till the vast head of the reptile emerged —its jaws bristling with fangs, and its dull eyes fixing themselves hungrily on the spot where I sat

motionless. And now its fore feet were on the
strand—now its enormous breast, scaled on either
side as in armour, in the centre showing corrugated
skin of a dull venomous yellow; and now its whole
length was on the land, a hundred feet or more
from the jaw to the tail. Another stride of those
ghastly feet would have brought it to the spot
where I sat. There was but a moment between me
and this grim form of death, when what seemed a
flash of lightning shot through the air, smote, and,
for a space in time briefer than that in which a
man can draw his breath, enveloped the monster;
and then, as the flash vanished, there lay before me
a blackened, charred, smouldering mass, a something gigantic, but of which even the outlines of
form were burned away, and rapidly crumbling into
dust and ashes. I remained still seated, still speech-
less, ice-cold with a new sensation of dread: what
had been horror was now awe.

I felt the child's hand on my head—fear left
me—the spell was broken—I rose up. "You see
with what ease the Vril-ya destroy their enemies,"
said Taë; and then, moving towards the bank, he

contemplated the smouldering relics of the monster, and said quietly, "I have destroyed larger creatures, but none with so much pleasure. Yes, it *is* a Krek; what suffering it must have inflicted while it lived!" Then he took up the poor fishes that had flung themselves ashore, and restored them mercifully to their native element.

CHAPTER XIX.

As we walked back to the town, Taë took a new and circuitous way, in order to show me what, to use a familiar term, I will call the 'Station,' from which emigrants or travellers to other communities commence their journeys. I had, on a former occasion, expressed a wish to see their vehicles. These I found to be of two kinds, one for land-journeys, one for aerial voyages: the former were of all sizes and forms, some not larger than an ordinary carriage, some movable houses of one story and containing several rooms, furnished according to the ideas of comfort or luxury which are entertained by the Vril-ya. The aerial vehicles were of light substances, not the least resembling our balloons, but rather our boats and pleasure-vessels, with helm and rudder, with large wings as paddles, and a central machine worked by vril. All the vehicles both for land or air were indeed worked by that potent and mysterious agency.

I saw a convoy set out on its journey, but it
had few passengers, containing chiefly articles of
merchandise, and was bound to a neighbouring
community; for among all the tribes of the Vril-ya
there is considerable commercial interchange. I
may here observe, that their money currency does
not consist of the precious metals, which are too
common among them for that purpose. The smaller
coins in ordinary use are manufactured from a peculiar fossil shell, the comparatively scarce remnant
of some very early deluge, or other convulsion of
nature, by which a species has become extinct. It
is minute, and flat as an oyster, and takes a jewel-
like polish. This coinage circulates among all the
tribes of the Vril-ya. Their larger transactions are
carried on much like ours, by bills of exchange,
and thin metallic plates which answer the purpose
of our bank-notes.

Let me take this occasion of adding that the
taxation among the tribe I became acquainted with
was very considerable, compared with the amount
of population. But I never heard that any one
grumbled at it, for it was devoted to purposes of

universal utility, and indeed necessary to the civilisation of the tribe. The cost of lighting so large a
range of country, of providing for emigration, of
maintaining the public buildings at which the various operations of national intellect were carried
on, from the first education of an infant to the departments in which the College of Sages were perpetually trying new experiments in mechanical
science: all these involved the necessity for considerable state funds. To these I must add an
item that struck me as very singular. I have said
that all the human labour required by the state is
carried on by children up to the marriageable age.
For this labour the state pays, and at a rate immeasurably higher than our remuneration to labour
even in the United States. According to their
theory, every child, male or female, on attaining the
marriageable age, and there terminating the period
of labour, should have acquired enough for an independent competence during life. As, no matter
what the disparity of fortune in the parents, all the
children must equally serve, so all are equally paid
according to their several ages or the nature of

their work. Where the parents or friends choose to retain a child in their own service, they must pay into the public fund in the same ratio as the state pays to the children it employs; and this sum is handed over to the child when the period of service expires. This practice serves, no doubt, to render the notion of social equality familiar and agreeable; and if it may be said that all the children form a democracy, no less truly it may be said that all the adults form an aristocracy. The exquisite politeness and refinement of manners among the Vril-ya, the generosity of their sentiments, the absolute leisure they enjoy for following out their own private pursuits, the amenities of their domestic intercourse, in which they seem as members of one noble order that can have no distrust of each other's word or deed, all combine to make the Vril-ya the most perfect nobility which a political disciple of Plato or Sidney could conceive for the ideal of an aristocratic republic.

CHAPTER XX.

FROM the date of the expedition with Taë which I have just narrated, the child paid me frequent visits. He had taken a liking to me, which I cordially returned. Indeed, as he was not yet twelve years old, and had not commenced the course of scientific studies with which childhood closes in that country, my intellect was less inferior to his than to that of the elder members of his race, especially of the Gy-ei, and most especially of the accomplished Zee. The children of the Vril-ya, having upon their minds the weight of so many active duties and grave responsibilities, are not generally mirthful; but Taë, with all his wisdom, had much of the playful good-humour one often finds the characteristic of elderly men of genius. He felt that sort of pleasure in my society which a boy of a similar age in the upper world has in the company of a pet dog or monkey. It amused him to try and teach me the ways of his people, as it amuses a nephew of mine to make his poodle walk on his hind legs or jump through a hoop. I willingly lent myself to such experiments, but I never achieved the success of the poodle. I was very much interested at first in the attempt to ply the wings which the youngest of the Vril-ya use as nimbly and easily as ours do their legs and arms; but my efforts were attended with contusions serious enough to make me abandon them in despair.

These wings, as I before said, are very large, reaching to the knee, and in repose thrown back so as to form a very graceful mantle. They are composed from the feathers of a gigantic bird that abounds in the rocky heights of the country—the colour mostly white, but sometimes with reddish streaks. They are fastened round the shoulders with light but strong springs of steel; and, when expanded, the arms slide through loops for that purpose, forming, as it were, a stout central membrane. As the arms are raised, a tubular lining beneath the vest or tunic becomes, by mechanical contrivance, inflated with air, increased or diminished at will by

the movement of the arms, and serving to buoy the
whole form as on bladders. The wings and the
balloon-like apparatus are highly charged with vril;
and when the body is thus wafted upward, it seems
to become singularly lightened of its weight. I
found it easy enough to soar from the ground; indeed, when the wings were spread it was scarcely
possible not to soar, but then came the difficulty
and the danger. I utterly failed in the power to use
and direct the pinions, though I am considered
among my own race unusually alert and ready in
bodily exercises, and am a very practised swimmer.
I could only make the most confused and blundering
efforts at flight. I was the servant of the wings; the
wings were not my servants—they were beyond my
control; and when by a violent strain of muscle, and,
I must fairly own, in that abnormal strength which
is given by excessive fright, I curbed their gyrations
and brought them near to the body, it seemed as if
I lost the sustaining power stored in them and the
connecting bladders, as when air is let out of a
balloon, and found myself precipitated again to
earth; saved, indeed, by some spasmodic flutterings,

from being dashed to pieces, but not saved from the bruises and the stun of a heavy fall. I would, however, have persevered in my attempts, but for the advice or the commands of the scientific Zee, who had benevolently accompanied my flutterings, and indeed, on the last occasion, flying just under me, received my form as it fell on her own expanded wings, and preserved me from breaking my head on the roof of the pyramid from which we had ascended.

"I see," she said, "that your trials are in vain, not from the fault of the wings and their appurtenances, nor from any imperfectness and malformation of your own corpuscular system, but from irremediable, because organic, defect in your power of volition. Learn that the connection between the will and the agencies of that fluid which has been subjected to the control of the Vril-ya was never established by the first discoverers, never achieved by a single generation; it has gone on increasing, like other properties of race, in proportion as it has been uniformly transmitted from parent to child, so that, at last, it has become an instinct; and an infant

13*

An of our race, wills to fly as intuitively and unconsciously as he wills to walk.   He thus plies his
invented or artificial wings with as much safety as
a bird plies those with which it is born.   I did not
think sufficiently of this when I allowed you to try
an experiment which allured me, for I longed to
have in you a companion.   I shall abandon the experiment now.   Your life is becoming dear to me."
Herewith the Gy's voice and face softened, and I
felt more seriously alarmed than I had been in my
previous flights.

Now that I am on the subject of wings, I ought
not to omit mention of a custom among the Gy-ei
which seems to me very pretty and tender in the
sentiment it implies.   A Gy wears wings habitually
while yet a virgin—she joins the Ana in their aerial
sports—she adventures alone and afar into the wilder
regions of the sunless world: in the boldness and
height of her soarings, not less than in the grace of
her movements, she excels the opposite sex.   But
from the day of marriage, she wears wings no more,
she suspends them with her own willing hand
over the nuptial couch, never to be resumed

unless the marriage tie be severed by divorce or death.

Now when Zee's voice and eyes thus softened —and at that softening I prophetically recoiled and shuddered—Taë, who had accompanied us in our flights, but who, child-like, had been much more amused with my awkwardness than sympathising in my fears or aware of my danger, hovered over us, posed amidst the still radiant air, serene and motionless on his outspread wings, and hearing the endearing words of the young Gy, laughed aloud. Said he, "If the Tish cannot learn the use of wings, you may still be his companion, Zee, for you can suspend your own."

CHAPTER XXI.

I HAD for some time observed in my host's highly informed and powerfully proportioned daughter that kindly and protective sentiment which, whether above the earth or below it, an all-wise Providence has bestowed upon the feminine division of the human race. But until very lately I had ascribed it to that affection for 'pets' which a human female at every age shares with a human child. I now became painfully aware that the feeling with which Zee deigned to regard me was different from that which I had inspired in Taë. But this conviction gave me none of that complacent gratification which the vanity of man ordinarily conceives from a flattering appreciation of his personal merits on the part of the fair sex; on the contrary, it inspired me with fear. Yet of all the Gy-ei in the community, if Zee were perhaps the wisest and the strongest, she was, by common repute, the gentlest, and she was certainly the most popularly beloved. The

desire to aid, to succour, to protect, to comfort, to
bless, seemed to pervade her whole being. Though
the complicated miseries that originate in penury
and guilt are unknown to the social system of the
Vril-ya, still, no sage had yet discovered in vril an
agency which could banish sorrow from life; and
wherever amongst her people sorrow found its way,
there Zee followed in the mission of comforter.
Did some sister Gy fail to secure the love she
sighed for? Zee sought her out, and brought all
the resources of her lore, and all the consolations
of her sympathy, to bear upon a grief that so needs
the solace of a confidant. In the rare cases, when
grave illness seized upon childhood or youth, and
the cases, less rare, when, in the hardy and adventurous probation of infants, some accident, attended with pain and injury occurred, Zee forsook
her studies and her sports, and became the healer
and the nurse. Her favourite flights were towards
the extreme boundaries of the domain where children were stationed on guard against outbreaks of
warring forces in nature, or the invasions of devouring animals, so that she might warn them of any

peril which her knowledge detected or foresaw, or
be at hand if any harm should befall. Nay, even
in the exercise of her scientific acquirements there
was a concurrent benevolence of purpose and will.
Did she learn any novelty in invention that would
be useful to the practitioner of some special art or
craft? she hastened to communicate and explain it.
Was some veteran sage of the College perplexed
and wearied with the toil of an abstruse study? she
would patiently devote herself to his aid, work out
details for him, sustain his spirits with her hopeful
smile, quicken his wit with her luminous suggestion,
be to him, as it were, his own good genius made
visible as the strengthener and inspirer. The same
tenderness she exhibited to the inferior creatures.
I have often known her bring home some sick and
wounded animal, and tend and cherish it as a
mother would tend and cherish her stricken child.
Many a time when I sat in the balcony, or hanging
garden, on which my window opened, I have
watched her rising in the air on her radiant wings,
and in a few moments groups of infants below,
catching sight of her, would soar upward with joy-

ous sounds of greeting; clustering and sporting around her, so that she seemed a very centre of innocent delight. When I have walked with her amidst the rocks and valleys without the city, the elk-deer would scent or see her from afar, come bounding up, eager for the caress of her hand, or follow her footsteps, till dismissed by some musical whisper that the creature had learned to comprehend. It is the fashion among the virgin Gy-ei to wear on their foreheads a circlet, or coronet, with gems resembling opals, arranged in four points or rays like stars. These are lustreless in ordinary use, but if touched by the vril wand they take a clear lambent flame, which illuminates, yet not burns. This serves as an ornament in their festivities, and as a lamp, if, in their wanderings beyond their artificial lights, they have to traverse the dark. There are times, when I have seen Zee's thoughtful majesty of face lighted up by this crowning halo, that I could scarcely believe her to be a creature of mortal birth, and bent my head before her as the vision of a being among the celestial orders. But never once did my heart feel for this lofty type of the noblest womanhood a sentiment of human love. Is it that, among the race I belong to, man's pride so far influences his passions that woman loses to him her special charm of woman if he feels her to be in all things eminently superior to himself? But by what strange infatuation could this peerless daughter of a race which, in the supremacy of its powers and the felicity of its conditions, ranked all other races in the category of barbarians, have deigned to honour me with her preference? In personal qualifications, though I passed for good-looking among the people I came from, the hand-somest of my countrymen might have seemed insignificant and homely beside the grand and serene type of beauty which characterised the aspect of the Vril-ya.

That novelty, the very difference between myself and those to whom Zee was accustomed, might serve to bias her fancy was probable enough, and as the reader will see later, such a cause might suffice to account for the predilection with which I was distinguished by a young Gy scarcely out of her childhood, and very inferior in all respects to

Zee. But whoever will consider those tender characteristics which I have just ascribed to the daughter of Aph-Lin, may readily conceive that the main cause of my attraction to her was in her instinctive desire to cherish, to comfort, to protect, and, in protecting, to sustain and to exalt. Thus, when I look back, I account for the only weakness unworthy of her lofty nature, which bowed the daughter of the Vril-ya to a woman's affection for one so inferior to herself as was her father's guest. But be the cause what it may, the consciousness that I had inspired such affection thrilled me with awe— a moral awe of her very perfections, of her mysterious powers, of the inseparable distinctions between her race and my own; and with that awe, I must confess to my shame, there combined the more material and ignoble dread of the perils to which her preference would expose me.

Could it be supposed for a moment that the parents and friends of this exalted being could view without indignation and disgust the possibility of an alliance between herself and a Tish? Her they could not punish, her they could not confine nor restrain. Neither in domestic nor in political life do they acknowledge any law of force amongst themselves; but they could effectually put an end to her infatuation by a flash of vril inflicted upon me.

Under these anxious circumstances, fortunately, my conscience and sense of honour were free from reproach. It became clearly my duty, if Zee's preference continued manifest, to intimate it to my host, with, of course, all the delicacy which is ever to be preserved by a well-bred man in confiding to another any degree of favour by which one of the fair sex may condescend to distinguish him. Thus, at all events, I should be freed from responsibility or suspicion of voluntary participation in the sentiments of Zee; and the superior wisdom of my host might probably suggest some sage extrication from my perilous dilemma. In this resolve I obeyed the ordinary instinct of civilised and moral man, who, erring though he be, still generally prefers the right course in those cases where it is obviously against his inclinations, his interests, and his safety to elect the wrong one.

CHAPTER XXII.

As the reader has seen, Aph-Lin had not favoured my general and unrestricted intercourse with his countrymen. Though relying on my promise to abstain from giving any information as to the world I had left, and still more on the promise of those to whom had been put the same request, not to question me, which Zee had exacted from Taë, yet he did not feel sure that, if I were allowed to mix with the strangers whose curiosity the sight of me had aroused, I could sufficiently guard myself against their inquiries. When I went out, therefore, it was never alone; I was always accompanied either by one of my host's family, or my child-friend Taë. Bra, Aph-Lin's wife, seldom stirred beyond the gardens which surrounded the house, and was fond of reading the ancient literature, which contained something of romance and adventure not to be found in the writings of recent ages, and presented pictures of a life unfamiliar to

her experience and interesting to her imagination;
pictures, indeed, of a life more resembling that
which we lead every day above ground, coloured
by our sorrows, sins, and passions, and much to
her what the Tales of the Genii or the Arabian
Nights are to us. But her love of reading did not
prevent Bra from the discharge of her duties as
mistress of the largest household in the city. She
went daily the round of the chambers, and saw
that the automata and other mechanical contrivances
were in order, that the numerous children employed
by Aph-Lin, whether in his private or public capacity, were carefully tended. Bra also inspected
the accounts of the whole estate, and it was her
great delight to assist her husband in the business
connected with his office as chief administrator of
the Lighting Department, so that her avocations
necessarily kept her much within doors. The two
sons were both completing their education at the
College of Sages; and the elder, who had a strong
passion for mechanics, and especially for works
connected with the machinery of timepieces and
automata, had decided in devoting himself to these

pursuits, and was now occupied in constructing a shop, or warehouse, at which his inventions could be exhibited and sold. The younger son preferred farming and rural occupations; and when not attending the College, at which he chiefly studied the theories of agriculture, was much absorbed by his practical application of that science to his father's lands. It will be seen by this how completely equality of ranks is established among this people —a shopkeeper being of exactly the same grade in estimation as the large landed proprietor. Aph-Lin was the wealthiest member of the community, and his eldest son preferred keeping a shop to any other avocation; nor was this choice thought to show any want of elevated notions on his part.

This young man had been much interested in examining my watch, the works of which were new to him, and was greatly pleased when I made him a present of it. Shortly after, he returned the gift with interest, by a watch of his own construction, marking both the time as in my watch and the time as kept among the Vril-ya. I have that watch still, and it has been much admired by many

among the most eminent watchmakers of London
and Paris. It is of gold, with diamond hands and
figures, and it plays a favourite tune among the
Vril-ya in striking the hours: it only requires to be
wound up once in ten months, and has never gone
wrong since I had it. These young brothers being
thus occupied, my usual companions in that family,
when I went abroad, were my host or his daughter.
Now, agreeably with the honourable conclusions I
had come to, I began to excuse myself from Zee's
invitations to go out alone with her, and seized an
occasion when that learned Gy was delivering a
lecture at the College of Sages to ask Aph-Lin to
show me his country-seat. As this was at some
little distance, and as Aph-Lin was not fond of
walking, while I had discreetly relinquished all attempts at flying, we proceeded to our destination
in one of the aerial boats belonging to my host.
A child of eight years old, in his employ, was our
conductor. My host and myself reclined on cushions, and I found the movement very easy and
luxurious.

"Aph-Lin," said I, "you will not, I trust, be dis-

pleased with me, if I ask your permission to travel
for a short time, and visit other tribes or communities of your illustrious race. I have also a
strong desire to see those nations which do not
adopt your institutions, and which you consider as
savages. It would interest me greatly to notice
what are the distinctions between them and the
races whom we consider civilised in the world I
have left."

"It is utterly impossible that you should go
hence alone," said Aph-Lin. "Even among the
Vril-ya you would be exposed to great dangers.
Certain peculiarities of formation and colour, and
the extraordinary phenomenon of hirsute bushes
upon your cheeks and chin, denoting in you a
species of An distinct alike from our race and any
known race of barbarians yet extant, would attract,
of course, the special attention of the College of
Sages in whatever community of Vril-ya you visited,
and it would depend upon the individual temper
of some individual sage whether you would be received, as you have been here, hospitably, or
whether you would not be at once dissected for

scientific purposes. Know that when the Tur first
took you to his house, and while you were there
put to sleep by Taë in order to recover from your
previous pain or fatigue, the sages summoned by
the Tur were divided in opinion whether you were
a harmless or an obnoxious animal. During your
unconscious state your teeth were examined, and
they clearly showed that you were not only gramin-
ivorous, but carnivorous. Carnivorous animals of
your size are always destroyed, as being of dangerous and savage nature. Our teeth, as you have
doubtless observed,* are not those of the creatures
who devour flesh. It is, indeed, maintained by Zee
and other philosophers, that as, in remote ages, the
Ana did prey upon living beings of the brute
species, their teeth must have been fitted for that
purpose. But, even if so, they have been modified
by hereditary transmission, and suited to the food
on which we now exist; nor are even the barbarians,
who adopt the turbulent and ferocious institutions
of Glek-Nas, devourers of flesh like beasts of prey.

* I never had observed it; and, if I had, am not physiologist enough
to have distinguished the difference.

"In the course of this dispute it was proposed to dissect you; but Taë begged you off, and the Tur being, by office, averse to all novel experiments at variance with our custom of sparing life, except where it is clearly proved to be for the good of the community to take it, sent to me, whose business it is, as the richest man of the state, to afford hospitality to strangers from a distance. It was at my option to decide whether or not you were a stranger whom I could safely admit. Had I declined to receive you, you would have been handed over to the College of Sages, and what might there have befallen you I do not like to conjecture. Apart from this danger, you might chance to encounter some child of four years old, just put in possession of his vril staff; and who, in alarm at your strange appearance, and in the impulse of the moment, might reduce you to a cinder. Taë himself was about to do so when he first saw you, had his father not checked his hand. Therefore I say you cannot travel alone, but with Zee you would be safe; and I have no doubt that she would accompany you on a tour round the neighbouring

14*

communities of Vril-ya (to the savage states, No!):
I will ask her."

Now, as my main object in proposing to travel
was to escape from Zee, I hastily exclaimed, "Nay,
pray do not! I relinquish my design. You have
said enough as to its dangers to deter me from it;
and I can scarcely think it right that a young Gy
of the personal attractions of your lovely daughter
should travel into other regions without a better
protector than a Tish of my insignificant strength
and stature."

Aph-Lin emitted the soft sibilant sound which
is the nearest approach to laughter that a full-
grown An permits to himself, ere he replied:
"Pardon my discourteous but momentary indul-
gence of mirth at any observation seriously made
by my guest. I could not but be amused at the
idea of Zee, who is so fond of protecting others
that children call her 'THE GUARDIAN,' needing a
protector herself against any dangers arising from
the audacious admiration of males. Know that
our Gy-ei, while unmarried, are accustomed to
travel alone among other tribes, to see if they find

there some An who may please them more than the Ana they find at home. Zee has already made three such journeys, but hitherto her heart has been untouched."

Here the opportunity which I sought was afforded to me, and I said, looking down, and with faltering voice, "Will you, my kind host, promise to pardon me, if what I am about to say gives you offence?"

"Say only the truth, and I cannot be offended; or, could I be so, it would be not for me, but for you to pardon."

"Well, then, assist me to quit you, and, much as I should have liked to witness more of the wonders, and enjoy more of the felicity, which belong to your people, let me return to my own."

"I fear there are reasons why I cannot do that; at all events, not without permission of the Tur, and he, probably, would not grant it. You are not destitute of intelligence; you may (though I do not think so) have concealed the degree of destructive powers possessed by your people; you might, in short, bring upon us some danger; and if the

Tur entertains that idea, it would clearly be his duty either to put an end to you, or enclose you in a cage for the rest of your existence. But why should you wish to leave a state of society which you so politely allow to be more felicitous than your own?"

"Oh, Aph-Lin! my answer is plain. Lest in aught, and unwittingly, I should betray your hospitality; lest, in that caprice of will which in our world is proverbial among the other sex, and from which even a Gy is not free, your adorable daughter should deign to regard me, though a Tish, as if I were a civilised An, and—and—and——"

"Court you as her spouse," put in Aph-Lin, gravely, and without any visible sign of surprise or displeasure.

"You have said it."

"That would be a misfortune," resumed my host, after a pause, "and I feel that you have acted as you ought in warning me. It is, as you imply, not uncommon for an unwedded Gy to conceive tastes as to the object she covets which appear whimsical to others; but there is no power to compel a young Gy to any course opposed to that which she chooses to pursue. All we can do is to reason with her, and experience tells us that the whole College of Sages would find it vain to reason with a Gy in a matter that concerns her choice in love. I grieve for you, because such a marriage would be against the A-glauran, or good of the community, for the children of such a marriage would adulterate the race: they might even come into the world with the teeth of carnivorous animals; this could not be allowed: Zee, as a Gy, cannot be controlled; but you, as a Tish, can be destroyed. I advise you, then, to resist her addresses; to tell her plainly that you can never return her love. This happens constantly. Many an An, however ardently wooed by one Gy, rejects her, and puts an end to her persecution by wedding another. The same course is open to you."

"No; for I cannot wed another Gy without equally injuring the community, and exposing it to the chance of rearing carnivorous children."

"That is true. All I can say, and I say it with

the tenderness due to a Tish, and the respect due
to a guest, is frankly this—if you yield, you will
become a cinder. I must leave it to you to take
the best way you can to defend yourself. Perhaps
you had better tell Zee that she is ugly. That assurance on the lips of him she woos generally suf-
fices to chill the most ardent Gy. Here we are at
my country-house."

CHAPTER XXIIL

I CONFESS that my conversation with Aph-Lin, and the extreme coolness with which he stated his inability to control the dangerous caprice of his daughter, and treated the idea of the reduction into a cinder to which her amorous flame might expose my too seductive person, took away the pleasure I should otherwise have had in the contemplation of my host's country-seat, and the astonishing perfection of the machinery by which his farming operations were conducted. The house differed in appearance from the massive and sombre building which Aph-Lin inhabited in the city, and which seemed akin to the rocks out of which the city itself had been hewn into shape. The walls of the country-seat were composed by trees placed a few feet apart from each other, the interstices being filled in with the transparent metallic substance which serves the purpose of glass among the Ana.

These trees were all in flower, and the effect was
very pleasing, if not in the best taste. We were
received at the porch by lifelike automata, who
conducted us into a chamber, the like to which I
never saw before, but have often on summer days
dreamily imagined. It was a bower—half room,
half garden. The walls were one mass of climbing
flowers. The open spaces, which we call windows,
and in which, here, the metallic surfaces were
slided back, commanded various views; some, of
the wide landscape with its lakes and rocks; some,
of small limited expanse answering to our con-
servatories, filled with tiers of flowers. Along the
sides of the room were flower-beds, interspersed
with cushions for repose. In the centre of the floor
was a cistern and a fountain of that liquid light
which I have presumed to be naphtha. It was
luminous and of a roseate hue; it sufficed without
lamps to light up the room with a subdued radiance.
All around the fountain was carpeted with a soft
deep lichen, not green (I have never seen that
colour in the vegetation of this country), but a
quiet brown, on which the eye reposes with the

same sense of relief as that with which in the upper
world it reposes on green. In the outlets upon
flowers (which I have compared to our conserva-
tories) there were singing-birds innumerable, which,
while we remained in the room, sang in those
harmonies of tune to which they are, in these parts,
so wonderfully trained. The roof was open. The
whole scene had charms for every sense—music
from the birds, fragrance from the flowers, and
varied beauty to the eye at every aspect. About
all was a voluptuous repose. What a place, me-
thought, for a honeymoon, if a Gy bride were a
little less formidably armed not only with the rights
of woman, but with the powers of man! but when
one thinks of a Gy, so learned, so tall, so stately,
so much above the standard of the creature we call
woman as was Zee, not even if I had felt no fear
of being reduced to a cinder, it is not of her I
should have dreamed in that bower so constructed
for dreams of poetic love.

The automata reappeared, serving one of those
delicious liquids which form the innocent wines of
the Vril-ya.

"Truly," said I, "this is a charming residence, and I can scarcely conceive why you do not settle yourself here instead of amid the gloomier abodes of the city."

"As responsible to the community for the administration of light, I am compelled to reside chiefly in the city, and can only come hither for short intervals."

"But since I understand from you that no honours are attached to your office, and it involves some trouble, why do you accept it?"

"Each of us obeys without question the command of the Tur. He said, 'Be it requested that Aph-Lin shall be Commissioner of Light,' so I had no choice; but having held the office now for a long time, the cares, which were at first unwelcome, have become, if not pleasing, at least endurable. We are all formed by custom—even the difference of our race from the savage is but the transmitted continuance of custom, which becomes, through hereditary descent, part and parcel of our nature. You see there are Ana who even reconcile themselves to the responsibilities of chief magistrate, but no one would do so if his duties had not been rendered so light, or if there were any questions as to compliance with his requests."

"Not even if you thought the requests unwise or unjust?"

"We do not allow ourselves to think so, and, indeed, everything goes on as if each and all governed themselves according to immemorial custom."

"When the chief magistrate dies or retires, how do you provide for his successor?"

"The An who has discharged the duties of chief magistrate for many years is the best person to choose one by whom those duties may be understood, and he generally names his successor."

"His son, perhaps?"

"Seldom that; for it is not an office any one desires or seeks, and a father naturally hesitates to constrain his son. But if the Tur himself decline to make a choice, for fear it might be supposed that he owed some grudge to the person on whom his choice would settle, then there are three of the College of Sages who draw lots among themselves which shall have the power to elect the chief. We consider that the judgment of one An of ordinary capacity is better than the judgment of three or more, however wise they may be; for among three there would probably be disputes; and where there are disputes, passion clouds judgment. The worst choice made by one who has no motive in choosing wrong, is better than the best choice made by many who have many motives for not choosing right."

"You reverse in your policy the maxims adopted in my country."

"Are you all, in your country, satisfied with your governors?"

"All! certainly not; the governors that most please some are sure to be those most displeasing to others."

"Then our system is better than yours."

"For you it may be; but according to our system a Tish could not be reduced to a cinder if a female compelled him to marry her; and as a Tish I sigh to return to my native world."

"Take courage, my dear little guest; Zee can't

compel you to marry her. She can only entice you
to do so. Don't be enticed. Come and look round
my domain."

We went forth into a close, bordered with sheds;
for though the Ana keep no stock for food, there
are some animals which they rear for milking and
others for shearing. The former have no resemblance to our cows, nor the latter to our sheep,
nor do I believe such species exist amongst them.
They use the milk of three varieties of animal: one
resembles the antelope, but is much larger, being
as tall as a camel; the other two are smaller, and,
though differing somewhat from each other, resemble
no creature I ever saw on earth. They are very
sleek and of rounded proportions; their colour that
of the dappled deer,' with very mild countenances
and beautiful dark eyes. The milk of these three
creatures differs in richness and in taste. It is
usually diluted with water, and flavoured with the
juice of a peculiar and perfumed fruit, and in itself
is very nutritious and palatable. The animal whose
fleece serves them for clothing and many other purposes, is more like the Italian she-goat than any

other creature, but is considerably larger, has no
horns, and is free from the displeasing odour of
our goats. Its fleece is not thick, but very long
and fine; it varies in colour, but is never white,
more generally of a slate-like or lavender hue. For
clothing it is usually worn dyed to suit the taste of
the wearer. These animals were exceedingly tame,
and were treated with extraordinary care and affection by the children (chiefly female) who tended
them.

We then went through vast storehouses filled
with grains and fruits. I may here observe that
the main staple of food among these people consists—firstly, of a kind of corn much larger in ear
than our wheat, and which by culture is perpetually
being brought into new varieties of flavour; and,
secondly, of a fruit of about the size of a small
orange, which, when gathered, is hard and bitter.
It is stowed away for many months in their warehouses, and then becomes succulent and tender. Its
juice, which is of dark-red colour, enters into most
of their sauces. They have many kinds of fruit of
the nature of the olive, from which delicious oils

are extracted. They have a plant somewhat resembling the sugar-cane, but its juices are less
sweet and of a delicate perfume. They have no
bees nor honey-kneading insects, but they make
much use of a sweet gum that oozes from a conifer-
ous plant, not unlike the araucaria. Their soil
teems also with esculent roots and vegetables, which
it is the aim of their culture to improve and vary
to the utmost. And I never remember any meal
among this people, however it might be confined
to the family household, in which some delicate
novelty in such articles of food was not introduced.
In fine, as I before observed, their cookery is exquisite, so diversified and nutritious that one does
not miss animal food; and their own physical forms
suffice to show that with them, at least, meat is not
required for superior production of muscular fibre.
They have no grapes—the drinks extracted from
their fruits are innocent and refreshing. Their
staple beverage, however, is water, in the choice
of which they are very fastidious, distinguishing at
once the slightest impurity.

"My younger son takes great pleasure in aug-

menting our produce," said Aph-Lin as we passed
through the storehouses, "and therefore will inherit
these lands, which constitute the chief part of my
wealth. To my elder son such inheritance would
be a great trouble and affliction."

"Are there many sons among you who think
the inheritance of vast wealth would be a great
trouble and affliction?"

"Certainly; there are indeed very few of the
Vril-ya who do not consider that a fortune much
above the average is a heavy burden. We are
rather a lazy people after the age of childhood, and
do not like undergoing more cares than we can
help, and great wealth does give its owner many
cares. For instance, it marks us out for public
offices, which none of us like and none of us can
refuse. It necessitates our taking a continued interest in the affairs of any of our poorer countrymen, so that we may anticipate their wants and
see that none fall into poverty. There is an old
proverb amongst us which says, 'The poor man's
need is the rich man's shame——'"

"Pardon me, if I interrupt you for a moment.

You then allow that some, even of the Vril-ya,
know want, and need relief?"

"If by want you mean the destitution that pre-
vails in a Koom-Posh, *that* is impossible with us,
unless an An has, by some extraordinary process,
got rid of all his means, cannot or will not emigrate,
and has either tired out the affectionate aid of his
relations or personal friends, or refuses to accept it."

"Well, then, does he not supply the place of
an infant or automaton, and become a labourer—
a servant?"

"No; then we regard him as an unfortunate
person of unsound reason, and place him, at the
expense of the State, in a public building, where
every comfort and every luxury that can mitigate
his affliction are lavished upon him. But an An
does not like to be considered out of his mind,
and therefore such cases occur so seldom that the
public building I speak of is now a deserted ruin,
and the last inmate of it was an An whom I recol-
lect to have seen in my childhood. He did not
seem conscious of loss of reason, and wrote glaubs

15*

(poetry). When I spoke of wants, I meant such
wants as an An with desires larger than his means
sometimes entertains—for expensive singing-birds,
or bigger houses, or country-gardens; and the obvious way to satisfy such wants is to buy of him
something that he sells. Hence Ana like myself,
who are very rich, are obliged to buy a great many
things they do not require, and live on a very large
scale where they might prefer to live on a small
one. For instance, the great size of my house in
the town is a source of much trouble to my wife,
and even to myself; but I am compelled to have it
thus incommodiously large, because, as the richest
An of the community, I am appointed to entertain
the strangers from the other communities when they
visit us, which they do in great crowds twice a-year,
when certain periodical entertainments are held,
and when relations scattered throughout all the
realms of the Vril-ya joyfully reunite for a time.
This hospitality, on a scale so extensive, is not to
my taste, and therefore I should have been happier
had I been less rich. But we must all bear the lot
assigned to us in this short passage through time

that we call life. After all, what are a hundred years, more or less, to the ages through which we must pass hereafter! Luckily, I have one son who likes great wealth. It is a rare exception to the general rule, and I own I cannot myself understand it."

After this conversation I sought to return to the subject which continued to weigh on my heart—viz., the chances of escape from Zee. But my host politely declined to renew that topic, and summoned our air-boat. On our way back we were met by Zee, who, having found us gone, on her return from the College of Sages, had unfurled her wings and flown in search of us.

Her grand, but to me unalluring, countenance brightened as she beheld me, and, poising herself beside the boat on her large outspread plumes, she said reproachfully to Aph-Lin—"Oh, father, was it right in you to hazard the life of your guest in a vehicle to which he is so unaccustomed? He might, by an incautious movement, fall over the side; and, alas! he is not like us, he has no wings. It were death to him to fall. Dear one!" (she added, accosting my shrinking self in a softer voice), "have you no thought of me, that you should thus hazard a life which has become almost a part of mine? Never again be thus rash, unless I am thy companion. What terror thou hast stricken into me!"

I glanced furtively at Aph-Lin, expecting, at least, that he would indignantly reprove his daughter for expressions of anxiety and affection, which, under all the circumstances, would, in the world above ground, be considered immodest in the lips of a young female, addressed to a male not affianced to her, even if of the same rank as herself.

But so confirmed are the rights of females in that region, and so absolutely foremost among those rights do females claim the privilege of courtship, that Aph-Lin would no more have thought of reproving his virgin daughter, than he would have thought of disobeying the Tur. In that country, custom, as he implied, is all and all.

He answered mildly, "Zee, the Tish was in no danger, and it is my belief that he can take very good care of himself."

"I would rather that he let me charge myself

with his care. Oh, heart of my heart, it was in the thought of thy danger that I first felt how much I loved thee!"

Never did man feel in so false a position as I did. These words were spoken loud in the hearing of Zee's father—in the hearing of the child who steered. I blushed with shame for them, and for her, and could not help replying angrily: "Zee, either you mock me, which, as your father's guest, misbecomes you, or the words you utter are improper for a maiden Gy to address even to an An of her own race, if he has not wooed her with the consent of her parents. How much more improper to address them to a Tish, who has never presumed to solicit your affections, and who can never regard you with other sentiments than those of reverence and awe!"

Aph-Lin made me a covert sign of approbation, but said nothing.

"Be not so cruel!" exclaimed Zee, still in sonorous accents. "Can love command itself where it is truly felt! Do you suppose that a maiden Gy

will conceal a sentiment that it elevates her to
feel! What a country you must have come from!"

Here Aph-Lin gently interposed, saying, "Among
the Tish-a the rights of your sex do not appear to
be established, and at all events my guest may converse with you more freely if unchecked by the
presence of others."

To this remark Zee made no reply, but, darting
on me a tender reproachful glance, agitated her
wings and fled homeward.

"I had counted, at least, on some aid from my
host," said I, bitterly, "in the perils to which his
own daughter exposes me."

"I gave you the best aid I could. To contra-
dict a Gy in her love affairs is to confirm her purpose. She allows no counsel to come between her
and her affections."

———

CHAPTER XXIV.

On alighting from the air-boat, a child accosted Aph-Lin in the hall with a request that he would be present at the funeral obsequies of a relation who had recently departed from that nether world.

Now, I had never seen a burial-place or cemetery amongst this people, and, glad to seize even so melancholy an occasion to defer an encounter with Zee, I asked Aph-Lin if I might be permitted to witness with him the interment of his relation; unless, indeed, it were regarded as one of those sacred ceremonies to which a stranger to their race might not be admitted.

"The departure of an An to a happier world," answered my host, "when, as in the case of my kinsman, he has lived so long in this as to have lost pleasure in it, is rather a cheerful though quiet festival than a sacred ceremony, and you may accompany me if you will."

Preceded by the child-messenger, we walked up the main street to a house at some little distance, and, entering the hall, were conducted to a room on the ground-floor, where we found several persons assembled round a couch on which was laid the deceased. It was an old man, who had, as I was told, lived beyond his 130th year. To judge by the calm smile on his countenance, he had passed away without suffering. One of the sons, who was now the head of the family, and who seemed in vigorous middle life, though he was considerably more than seventy, stepped forward with a cheerful face and told Aph-Lin "that the day before he died his father had seen in a dream his departed Gy, and was eager to be reunited to her, and restored to youth beneath the nearer smile of the All-Good."

While these two were talking, my attention was drawn to a dark metallic substance at the farther end of the room. It was about twenty feet in length, narrow in proportion, and all closed round, save, near the roof, there were small round holes through which might be seen a red light. From

the interior emanated a rich and sweet perfume;
and while I was conjecturing what purpose this
machine was to serve, all the time-pieces in the
town struck the hour with their solemn musical
chime; and as that sound ceased, music of a more
joyous character, but still of a joy subdued and
tranquil, rang throughout the chamber, and from
the walls beyond, in a choral peal. Symphonious
with the melody, those present lifted their voices
in chant. The words of this hymn were simple.
They expressed no regret, no farewell, but rather a
greeting to the new world whither the deceased had
preceded the living. Indeed, in their language, the
funeral hymn is called the 'Birth Song.' Then the
corpse, covered by a long cerement, was tenderly
lifted up by six of the nearest kinsfolk and borne
towards the dark thing I have described. I pressed
forward to see what happened. A sliding door or
panel at one end was lifted up—the body deposited
within, on a shelf—the door reclosed—a spring at
the side touched—a sudden *whishing*, sighing sound
heard from within; and lo! at the other end of the
machine the lid fell down, and a small handful of

smouldering dust dropped into a *patera* placed to
receive it. The son took up the *patera* and said
(in what I understood afterwards was the usual
form of words), "Behold how great is the Maker!
To this little dust He gave form and life and soul.
It needs not this little dust for Him to renew form
and life and soul to the beloved one we shall soon
see again."

Each present bowed his head and pressed his
hand to his heart. Then a young female child
opened a small door within the wall, and I perceived, in the recess, shelves on which were placed
many *patera* like that which the son held, save that
they all had covers. With such a cover a Gy now
approached the son, and placed it over the cup, on
which it closed with a spring. On the lid were
engraven the name of the deceased, and these
words:—"Lent to us" (here the date of birth).
"Recalled from us" (here the date of death.)

The closed door shut with a musical sound, and
all was over.

CHAPTER XXV.

"AND this," said I, with my mind full of what I had witnessed—"this, I presume, is your usual form of burial?"

"Our invariable form," answered Aph-Lin. "What is it amongst your people?"

"We inter the body whole within the earth."

"What! to degrade the form you have loved and honoured, the wife on whose breast you have slept, to the loathsomeness of corruption?"

"But if the soul lives again, can it matter whether the body waste within the earth or is reduced by that awful mechanism, worked, no doubt by the agency of vril, into a pinch of dust?"

"You answer well," said my host, "and there is no arguing on a matter of feeling; but to me your custom is horrible and repulsive, and would serve to invest death with gloomy and hideous associations. It is something, too, to my mind, to

be able to preserve the token of what has been our
kinsman or friend within the abode in which we
live. We thus feel more sensibly that he still lives,
though not visibly so to us. But our sentiments in
this, as in all things, are created by custom. Custom
is not to be changed by a wise An, any more than
it is changed by a wise Community, without the
gravest deliberation, followed by the most earnest
conviction. It is only thus that change ceases to
be changeability, and once made is made for
good."

When we regained the house, Aph-Lin summoned
some of the children in his service and sent them
round to several of his friends, requesting their at-
tendance that day, during the Easy Hours, to a
festival in honour of his kinsman's recall to the All-
Good. This was the largest and gayest assembly I
ever witnessed during my stay among the Ana, and
was prolonged far into the Silent Hours.

The banquet was spread in a vast chamber reserved especially for grand occasions. This differed
from our entertainments, and was not without a
certain resemblance to those we read of in the

luxurious age of the Roman empire. There was
not one great table set out, but numerous small
tables, each appropriated to eight guests. It is considered that beyond that number conversation lan-
guishes and friendship cools. The Ana never laugh
loud, as I have before observed, but the cheerful
ring of their voices at the various tables betokened
gaiety of intercourse. As they have no stimulant
drinks, and are temperate in food, though so choice
and dainty, the banquet itself did not last long.
The tables sank through the floor, and then came
musical entertainments for those who liked them.
Many, however, wandered away:—some of the
younger ascended on their wings, for the hall was
roofless, forming aerial dances; others strolled through
the various apartments, examining the curiosities
with which they were stored, or formed themselves
into groups for various games, the favourite of which
is a complicated kind of chess played by eight
persons. I mixed with the crowd, but was prevented
joining in their conversation by the constant com-
panionship of one or the other of my host's sons,
appointed to keep me from obtrusive questionings.

The guests, however, noticed me but slightly; they had grown accustomed to my appearance, seeing me so often in the streets, and I had ceased to excite much curiosity.

To my great delight Zee avoided me, and evidently sought to excite my jealousy by marked attentions to a very handsome young An, who (though, as is the modest custom of the males when addressed by females, he answered with downcast eyes and blushing cheeks, and was demure and shy as young ladies new to the world are in most civilised countries, except England and America) was evidently much charmed by the tall Gy, and ready to falter a bashful "Yes" if she had actually proposed. Fervently hoping that she would, and more and more averse to the idea of reduction to a cinder after I had seen the rapidity with which a human body can be hurried into a pinch of dust, I amused myself by watching the manners of the other young people. I had the satisfaction of observing that Zee was no singular assertor of a female's most valued rights. Wherever I turned my eyes, or lent my ears, it seemed to me that the Gy was the woo-

ing party, and the An the coy and reluctant one.
The pretty innocent airs which an An gave himself
on being thus courted, the dexterity with which he
evaded direct answer to professions of attachment,
or turned into jest the flattering compliments ad·
dressed to him, would have done honour to the most
accomplished coquette. Both my male *chaperons*
were subjected greatly to these seductive influences,
and both acquitted themselves with wonderful honour
to their tact and self-control.

I said to the elder son, who preferred mechanical
employments to the management of a great property, and who was of an eminently philosophical
temperament,—"I find it difficult to conceive how
at your age, and with all the intoxicating effects on
the senses, of music and lights and perfumes, you
can be so cold to that impassioned Gy who
has just left you with tears in her eyes at your
cruelty."

The young An replied with a sigh, "Gentle Tish,
the greatest misfortune in life is to marry one Gy
if you are in love with another."

"Oh! you are in love with another!"

"Alas! yes."

"And she does not return your love?"

"I don't know. Sometimes a look, a tone, makes me hope so; but she has never plainly told me that she loves me."

"Have you not whispered in her own ear that you love her?"

"Fie! what are you thinking of? What world do you come from? Could I so betray the dignity of my sex? Could I be so un-Anly—so lost to shame, as to own love to a Gy who has not first owned hers to me?"

"Pardon: I was not quite aware that you pushed the modesty of your sex so far. But does no An ever say to a Gy, 'I love you,' till she says it first to him?"

"I can't say that no An has ever done so, but if he ever does, he is disgraced in the eyes of the Ana, and secretly despised by the Gy-ei. No Gy, well brought up, would listen to him; she would consider that he audaciously infringed on the rights of her sex, while outraging the modesty which dignifies his own. It is very provoking," continued the An, "for she whom I love has certainly courted no one else, and I cannot but think she likes me. Sometimes I suspect that she does not court me because she fears I would ask some unreasonable settlement as to the surrender of her rights. But if so, she cannot really love me, for where a Gy really loves she foregoes all rights."

"Is this young Gy present?"

"Oh yes. She sits yonder talking to my mother."

I looked in the direction to which my eyes were thus guided, and saw a Gy dressed in robes of bright red, which among this people is a sign that a Gy as yet prefers a single state. She wears grey, a neutral tint, to indicate that she is looking about for a spouse; dark purple if she wishes to intimate that she has made a choice; purple and orange when she is betrothed or married; light blue when she is divorced or a widow and would marry again. Light blue is of course seldom seen.

Among a people where all are of so high a type of beauty, it is difficult to single out one as peculiarly handsome. My young friend's choice seemed

to me to possess the average of good looks; but
there was an expression in her face that pleased me
more than did the faces of the young Gy-ei generally,
because it looked less bold—less conscious of female
rights. I observed that, while she talked to Bra,
she glanced, from time to time, sidelong at my
young friend.

"Courage," said I; "that young Gy loves you."

"Ay, but if she will not say so, how am I the
better for her love?"

"Your mother is aware of your attachment?"

"Perhaps so. I never owned it to her. It would
be un-Anly to confide such weakness to a mother.
I have told my father; he may have told it again to
his wife."

"Will you permit me to quit you for a moment
and glide behind your mother and your beloved?
I am sure they are talking about you. Do not
hesitate. I promise that I will not allow myself to
be questioned till I rejoin you."

The young An pressed his hand on his heart,
touched me lightly on the head, and allowed me to

quit his side. I stole unobserved behind his mother and his beloved. I overheard their talk.

Bra was speaking; said she, "There can be no doubt of this: either my son, who is of marriageable age, will be decoyed into marriage with one of his many suitors, or he will join those who emigrate to a distance and we shall see him no more. If you really care for him, my dear Lo, you should propose."

"I do care for him, Bra; but I doubt if I could really ever win his affection. He is fond of his inventions and timepieces; and I am not like Zee, but so dull that I fear I could not enter into his favourite pursuits, and then he would get tired of me, and at the end of three years divorce me, and I could never marry another—never."

"It is not necessary to know about timepieces to know how to be so necessary to the happiness of an An, who cares for timepieces that he would rather give up the timepieces than divorce his Gy. You see, my dear Lo," continued Bra, "that precisely because we are the stronger sex, we rule the other, provided we never show our strength. If you were

superior to my son in making timepieces and automata, you should, as his wife, always let him suppose you thought him superior in that art to yourself. The An tacitly allows the pre-eminence of the
Gy in all except his own special pursuit. But if
she either excels him in that, or affects not to ad-
mire him for his proficiency in it, he will not love
her very long; perhaps he may even divorce her.
But where a Gy really loves, she soon learns to
love all that the An does."

The young Gy made no answer to this address.
She looked down musingly, then a smile crept
over her lips, and she rose, still silent, and went
through the crowd till she paused by the young
An who loved her. I followed her steps, but discreetly stood at a little distance while I watched
them. Somewhat to my surprise, till I recollected
the coy tactics among the Ana, the lover seemed
to receive her advances with an air of indifference. He even moved away, but she pursued
his steps, and, a little time after, both spread their
wings and vanished amid the luminous space
above.

Just then I was accosted by the chief magistrate, who mingled with the crowd distinguished by no signs of deference or homage. It so happened that I had not seen this great dignitary since the day I had entered his dominions, and recalling Aph-Lin's words as to his terrible doubt whether or not I should be dissected, a shudder crept over me at the sight of his tranquil countenance.

"I hear much of you, stranger, from my son Taë," said the Tur, laying his hand politely on my bended head. "He is very fond of your society, and I trust you are not displeased with the customs of our people."

I muttered some unintelligible answer, which I intended to be an assurance of my gratitude for the kindness I had received from the Tur, and my admiration of his countrymen, but the dissecting-knife gleamed before my mind's eye and choked my utterance. A softer voice said, "My brother's friend must be dear to me." And looking up I saw a young Gy, who might be sixteen years old,

standing beside the magistrate and gazing at me
with a very benignant countenance. She had not
come to her full growth, and was scarcely taller
than myself (viz., about 5 feet 10 inches), and,
thanks to that comparatively diminutive stature,
I thought her the loveliest Gy I had hitherto seen.
I suppose something in my eyes revealed that
impression, for her countenance grew yet more
benignant.

"Taë tells me," she said, "that you have not
yet learned to accustom yourself to wings. That
grieves me, for I should have liked to fly with
you."

"Alas!" I replied, "I can never hope to enjoy
that happiness. I am assured by Zee that the safe
use of wings is a hereditary gift, and it would take
generations before one of my race could poise
himself in the air like a bird."

"Let not that thought vex you too much,"
replied this amiable Princess, "for, after all, there
must come a day when Zee and myself must resign
our wings for ever. Perhaps when that day comes

we might be glad if the An we chose was also without wings."

The Tur had left us, and was lost amongst the crowd. I began to feel at ease with Taë's charming sister, and rather startled her by the boldness of my compliment in replying "that no An she could choose would ever use his wings to fly away from her." It is so against custom for an An to say such civil things to a Gy till she has declared her passion for him, and been accepted as his betrothed, that the young maiden stood quite dumbfounded for a few moments. Nevertheless she did not seem displeased. At last recovering herself, she invited me to accompany her into one of the less crowded rooms and listen to the songs of the birds. I followed her steps as she glided before me, and she led me into a chamber almost deserted. A fountain of naphtha was playing in the centre of the room; round it were ranged soft divans, and the walls of the room were open on one side to an aviary in which the birds were chanting their artful chorus. The Gy seated herself on one of the divans, and I placed myself at her side. "Taē tells me," she said, "that Aph-Lin has made it the law * of his house that you are not to be questioned as to the country you come from or the reason why you visit us. Is it so?"

"It is."

"May I, at least, without sinning against that law, ask at least if the Gy-ei in your country are of the same pale colour as yourself, and no taller?"

"I do not think, O beautiful Gy, that I infringe the law of Aph-Lin, which is more binding on myself than any one, if I answer questions so innocent. The Gy-ei in my country are much fairer of hue than I am, and their average height is at least a head shorter than mine."

"They cannot then be so strong as the Ana amongst you? But I suppose their superior vril force makes up for such extraordinary disadvantage of size?"

---

* Literally "has said, In this house be it requested." Words synonymous with law, as implying forcible obligation, are avoided by this singular people. Even had it been decreed by the Tur that his College of Sages should dissect me, the decree would have run blandly thus,—"Be it requested that, for the good of the community, the carnivorous Tish be requested to submit himself to dissection."

"They do not profess the vril force as you know it. But still they are very powerful in my country, and an An has small chance of a happy life if he be not more or less governed by his Gy."

"You speak feelingly," said Taë's sister, in a tone of voice half sad, half petulant. "You are married, of course!"

"No—certainly not."

"Nor betrothed!"

"Nor betrothed."

"Is it possible that no Gy has proposed to you!"

"In my country the Gy does not propose; the An speaks first."

"What a strange reversal of the laws of nature!" said the maiden, "and what want of modesty in your sex! But have you never proposed, never loved one Gy more than another!"

I felt embarrassed by these ingenuous questionings, and said, "Pardon me, but I think we are beginning to infringe upon Aph-Lin's injunction. Thus much only will I say in answer, and then, I

implore you, ask no more. I did once feel the
preference you speak of; I did propose, and the
Gy would willingly have accepted me, but her
parents refused their consent."

"Parents! Do you mean seriously to tell me
that parents can interfere with the choice of their
daughters?"

"Indeed they can, and do very often."

"I should not like to live in that country," said
the Gy, simply; "but I hope you will never go back
to it."

I bowed my head in silence. The Gy gently
raised my face with her right hand, and looked
into it tenderly. "Stay with us," she said; "stay
with us, and be loved."

What I might have answered, what dangers of
becoming a cinder I might have encountered, I
still tremble to think, when the light of the naphtha
fountain was obscured by the shadow of wings; and
Zee, flying through the open roof, alighted beside
us. She said not a word, but, taking my arm with
her mighty hand, she drew me away, as a mother
draws a naughty child, and led me through the

apartments to one of the corridors, on which, by
the mechanism they generally prefer to stairs, we
ascended to my own room. This gained, Zee
breathed on my forehead, touched my breast with
her staff, and I was instantly plunged into a profound sleep.

When I awoke some hours later, and heard
the song of the birds in the adjoining aviary, the
remembrance of Taë's sister, her gentle looks and
caressing words, vividly returned to me; and so
impossible is it for one born and reared in our
upper world's state of society to divest himself
of ideas dictated by vanity and ambition, that I
found myself instinctively building proud castles
in the air.

"Tish though I be," thus ran my meditations
—"Tish though I be, it is then clear that Zee is
not the only Gy whom my appearance can capti-
vate. Evidently I am loved by a PRINCESS, the
first maiden of this land, the daughter of the absolute Monarch whose autocracy they so idly seek to
disguise by the republican title of chief magistrate.
But for the sudden swoop of that horrible Zee,

this Royal Lady would have formally proposed to
me; and though it may be very well for Aph-Lin,
who is only a subordinate minister, a mere Commissioner of Light, to threaten me with destruction if I accept his daughter's hand, yet a
Sovereign, whose word is law, could compel the
community to abrogate any custom that forbids
intermarriage with one of a strange race, and which
in itself is a contradiction to their boasted equality
of ranks.

"It is not to be supposed that his daughter,
who spoke with such incredulous scorn of the
interference of parents, would not have sufficient
influence with her Royal Father to save me from
the combustion to which Aph-Lin would condemn
my form. And if I were exalted by such an alliance, who knows but what the Monarch might elect
me as his successor. Why not? Few among this
indolent race of philosophers like the burden of
such greatness. All might be pleased to see the
supreme power lodged in the hands of an accomplished stranger who has experience of other and
livelier forms of existence; and, once chosen, what

reforms I would institute! What additions to the
really pleasant but too monotonous life of this
realm my familiarity with the civilised nations
above ground would effect! I am fond of the
sports of the field. Next to war, is not the chase a
king's pastime? In what varieties of strange game
does this nether world abound! How interesting
to strike down creatures that were known above
ground before the Deluge! But how? By that
terrible vril, in which, from want of hereditary
transmission, I could never be a proficient. No,
but by a civilised handy breech-loader, which these
ingenious mechanicians could not only make, but
no doubt improve; nay, surely I saw one in the
Museum. Indeed, as absolute king, I should dis-
countenance vril altogether, except in cases of war.
Apropos of war, it is perfectly absurd to stint a
people so intelligent, so rich, so well armed, to a
petty limit of territory sufficing for 10,000 or 12,000
families. Is not this restriction a mere philosophical
crotchet, at variance with the aspiring element in
human nature, such as has been partially, and with
complete failure, tried in the upper world by the

late Mr. Robert Owen. Of course one would not
go to war with neighbouring nations as well armed
as one's own subjects; but then, what of those regions inhabited by races unacquainted with vril,
and apparently resembling, in their democratic institutions, my American countrymen! One might
invade them without offence to the vril nations,
our allies, appropriate their territories, extending,
perhaps, to the most distant regions of the nether
earth, and thus rule over an empire in which the
sun never sets. (I forgot, in my enthusiasm, that
over those regions there was no sun to set.) As
for the fantastical notion against conceding fame
or renown to an eminent individual, because, for-
sooth, bestowal of honours insures contest in the
pursuit of them, stimulates angry passions, and
mars the felicity of peace—it is opposed to the
very elements, not only of the human but the brute
creation, which are all, if tamable, participators in
the sentiment of praise and emulation. What
renown would be given to a king who thus extended his empire! I should be deemed a demi-
god." Thinking of that, the other fanatical notion

of regulating this life by reference to one which, no doubt, we Christians firmly believe in, but never take into consideration, I resolved that enlightened philosophy compelled me to abolish a heathen religion so superstitiously at variance with modern thought and practical action. Musing over these various projects, I felt how much I should have liked at that moment to brighten my wits by a good glass of whisky-and-water. Not that I am habitually a spirit-drinker, but certainly there are times when a little stimulant of alcoholic nature, taken with a cigar, enlivens the imagination. Yes; certainly among these herbs and fruits there would be a liquid from which one could extract a pleasant vinous alcohol; and with a steak cut off one of those elks (ah! what offence to science to reject the animal food which our first medical men agree in recommending to the gastric juices of mankind!) one would certainly pass a more exhilarating hour of repast. Then, too, instead of those antiquated dramas performed by childish amateurs, certainly, when I am king, I will introduce our modern opera and a *corps de ballet*, for which one might find,

among the nations I shall conquer, young females
of less formidable height and thews than the Gy-ei
—not armed with vril, and not insisting upon one's
marrying them.

I was so completely rapt in these and similar
reforms, political, social, and moral, calculated to
bestow on the people of the nether world the
blessings of a civilisation known to the races of
the upper, that I did not perceive that Zee had
entered the chamber till I heard a deep sigh,
and, raising my eyes, beheld her standing by my
couch.

I need not say that, according to the manners
of this people, a Gy can, without indecorum, visit
an An in his chamber, though an An would be
considered forward and immodest to the last degree if he entered the chamber of a Gy without
previously obtaining her permission to do so. Fortunately I was in the full habiliments I had worn
when Zee had deposited me on the couch. Nevertheless I felt much irritated, as well as shocked,
by her visit, and asked in a rude tone what she
wanted.

"Speak gently, beloved one, I entreat you," said she, "for I am very unhappy. I have not slept since we parted."

"A due sense of your shameful conduct to me as your father's guest might well suffice to banish sleep from your eyelids. Where was the affection you pretend to have for me, where was even that politeness on which the Vril-ya pride themselves, when, taking advantage alike of that physical strength in which your sex, in this extraordinary region, excels our own, and of those detestable and unhallowed powers which the agencies of vril invest in your eyes and fingerends, you exposed me to humiliation before your assembled visitors, before Her Royal Highness—I mean, the daughter of your own chief magistrate,—carrying me off to bed like a naughty infant, and plunging me into sleep, without asking my consent!"

"Ungrateful! Do you reproach me for the evidences of my love! Can you think that, even if unstung by the jealousy which attends upon love till it fades away in blissful trust when we know that the heart we have wooed is won, I

17 *

could be indifferent to the perils to which the audacious overtures of that silly little child might expose you!"

"Hold! Since you introduce the subject of perils, it perhaps does not misbecome me to say that my most imminent perils come from yourself, or at least would come if I believed in your love and accepted your addresses. Your father has told me plainly that in that case I should be consumed into a cinder with as little compunction as if I were the reptile whom Taë blasted into ashes with the flash of his wand."

"Do not let that fear chill your heart to me," exclaimed Zee, dropping on her knees and absorbing my right hand in the space of her ample palm. "It is true, indeed, that we two cannot wed as those of the same race wed; true that the love between us must be pure as that which, in our belief, exists between lovers who reunite in the new life beyond that boundary at which the old life ends. But is it not happiness enough to be together, wedded in mind and in heart! Listen: I have just left my father. He consents to our union

on those terms. I have sufficient influence with
the College of Sages to insure their request to the
Tur not to interfere with the free choice of a Gy,
provided that her wedding with one of another race
be but the wedding of souls. Oh, think you that
true love needs ignoble union! It is not that I
yearn only . to be by your side in this life, to be
part and parcel of your joys and sorrows here: I
ask here for a tie which will bind us for ever and
for ever in the world of immortals. Do you reject
me!"

As she spoke, she knelt, and the whole character
of her face was changed; nothing of sternness left
to its grandeur; a divine light, as that of an immortal, shining out from its human beauty. But
she rather awed me as angel than moved me as
woman, and after an embarrassed pause, I faltered
forth evasive expressions of gratitude, and sought,
as delicately as I could, to point out how humiliat-
ing would be my position amongst her race in the
light of a husband who might never be permitted
the name of father.

"But," said Zee, "this community does not

constitute the whole world. No; nor do all the
populations comprised in the league of the Vril-ya.
For thy sake I will renounce my country and my
people. We will fly together to some region where
thou shalt be safe. I am strong enough to bear
thee on my wings across the deserts that intervene.
I am skilled enough to cleave open, amid the
rocks, valleys in which to build our home. Solitude
and a hut with thee would be to me society and
the universe. Or wouldst thou return to thine own
world, above the surface of this, exposed to the
uncertain seasons, and lit but by the changeful
orbs which constitute by thy description the fickle
character of those savage regions? If so, speak the
word, and I will force the way for thy return, so
that I am thy companion there, though, there as
here, but partner of thy soul, and fellow-traveller
with thee to the world in which there is no parting
and no death."

I could not but be deeply affected by the tenderness, at once so pure and so impassioned, with
which these words were uttered, and in a voice
that would have rendered musical the roughest

sounds in the rudest tongue. And for a moment it did occur to me that I might avail myself of Zee's agency to effect a safe and speedy return to the upper world. But a very brief space for reflection sufficed to show me how dishonourable and base a return for such devotion it would be to allure thus away, from her own people and a home in which I had been so hospitably treated, a creature to whom our world would be so abhorrent, and for whose barren, if spiritual love, I could not reconcile myself to renounce the more human affection of mates less exalted above my erring self. With this sentiment of duty towards the Gy combined another of duty towards the whole race I belonged to. Could I venture to introduce into the upper world a being so formidably gifted—a being that with a movement of her staff could in less than an hour reduce New York and its glorious Koom-Posh into a pinch of snuff? Rob her of one staff, with her science she could easily construct another; and with the deadly lightnings that armed the slender engine her whole frame was charged. If thus dangerous to the cities and

populations of the whole upper earth, could she be
a safe companion to myself in case her affection
should be subjected to change or embittered by
jealousy? These thoughts, which it takes so many
words to express, passed rapidly through my brain
and decided my answer.

"Zee," I said, in the softest tones I could command, and pressing respectful lips on the hand
into whose clasp mine had vanished—"Zee, I can
find no words to say how deeply I am touched,
and how highly I am honoured, by a love so dis-
interested and self-immolating. My best return to
it is perfect frankness. Each nation has its customs.
The customs of yours do not allow you to wed me;
the customs of mine are equally opposed to such a
union between those of races so widely differing.
On the other hand, though not deficient in courage
among my own people, or amid dangers with which
I am familiar, I cannot, without a shudder of horror,
think of constructing a bridal home in the heart
of some dismal chaos, with all the elements of
nature, fire and water and mephitic gases, at war
with each other, and with the probability that at

some moment, while you were busied in cleaving
rocks or conveying vril into lamps, I should be
devoured by a krek which your operations disturbed
from its hiding-place. I, a mere Tish, do not
deserve the love of a Gy, so brilliant, so learned,
so potent as yourself Yes, I do not deserve that
love, for I cannot return it."

Zee released my hand, rose to her feet, and
turned her face away to hide her emotions; then
she glided noiselessly along the room, and paused
at the threshold. Suddenly, impelled as by a new
thought, she returned to my side and said, in a
whispered tone,—

"You told me you would speak with perfect
frankness. With perfect frankness, then, answer me
this question. If you cannot love me, do you love
another?"

"Certainly, I do not."

"You do not love Tae's sister?"

"I never saw her before last night."

"That is no answer. Love is swifter than vril.
You hesitate to tell me. Do not think it is only
jealousy that prompts me to caution you. If the

Tur's daughter should declare love to you—if in
her ignorance she confides to her father any preference that may justify his belief that she will woo
you—he will have no option but to request your
immediate destruction, as he is specially charged
with the duty of consulting the good of the community, which could not allow a daughter of the
Vril-ya to wed a son of the Tish-a, in that sense of
marriage which does not confine itself to union of
the souls. Alas! there would then be for you no
escape. She has no strength of wing to uphold
you through the air; she has no science wherewith
to make a home in the wilderness. Believe that
here my friendship speaks, and that my jealousy is
silent."

With those words Zee left me. And recalling
those words, I thought no more of succeeding to
the throne of the Vril-ya, or of the political, social,
and moral reforms I should institute in the capacity
of Absolute Sovereign.

———

CHAPTER XXVI.

AFTER the conversation with Zee just recorded, I fell into a profound melancholy. The curious interest with which I had hitherto examined the life and habits of this marvellous community was at an end. I could not banish from my mind the consciousness that I was among a people who, however kind and courteous, could destroy me at any moment without scruple or compunction. The virtuous and peaceful life of the people which, while new to me, had seemed so holy a contrast to the contentions, the passions, the vices of the upper world, now began to oppress me with a sense of dulness and monotony. Even the serene tranquillity of the lustrous air preyed on my spirits. I longed for a change, even to winter, or storm, or darkness. I began to feel that, whatever our dreams of perfectibility, our restless aspirations towards a better, and higher, and calmer sphere of being, we, the mortals of the upper world, are not trained or fitted to enjoy for long the very happiness of which we dream or to which we aspire.

Now, in this social state of the Vril-ya, it was singular to mark how it contrived to unite and to harmonise into one system nearly all the objects which the various philosophers of the upper world have placed before human hopes as the ideals of a Utopian future. It was a state in which war, with all its calamities, was deemed impossible,—a state in which the freedom of all and each was secured to the uttermost degree, without one of those animosities which make freedom in the upper world depend on the perpetual strife of hostile parties. Here the corruption which debases democracies was as unknown as the discontents which undermine the thrones of monarchies. Equality here was not a name; it was a reality. Riches were not persecuted, because they were not envied. Here those problems connected with the labours of a working class, hitherto insoluble above ground, and above ground conducing to such bitterness between classes, were solved by a process the simplest,—a distinct and separate working class was dispensed with altogether. Mechanical inventions, constructed on principles that baffled my research to ascertain, worked by an agency infinitely more powerful and infinitely more easy of management than aught we have yet extracted from electricity or steam, with the aid of children whose strength was never overtasked, but who loved their employ- ment as sport and pastime, sufficed to create a Public-wealth so devoted to the general use that not a grumbler was ever heard of. The vices that rot our cities, here had no footing. Amusements abounded, but they were all innocent. No merry- makings conduced to intoxication, to riot, to disease. Love existed, and was ardent in pursuit, but its object, once secured, was faithful. The adulterer, the profligate, the harlot, were phenomena so un- known in this commonwealth, that even to find the words by which they were designated one would have had to search throughout an obsolete literature composed thousands of years before. They who have been students of theoretical philosophies, above ground, know that all these strange de- partures from civilised life do but realise ideas

which have been broached, canvassed, ridiculed,
contested for; sometimes partially tried, and still
put forth in fantastic books, but have never come
to practical result. Nor were these all the steps
towards theoretical perfectibility which this community had made. It had been the sober belief
of Descartes that the life of man could be prolonged, not, indeed, on this earth, to eternal
duration, but to what he called the age of the
patriarchs, and modestly defined to be from 100
to 150 years average length. Well, even this dream
of sages was here fulfilled—nay, more than fulfilled; for the vigour of middle life was preserved
even after the term of a century was passed. With
this longevity was combined a greater blessing than
itself—that of continuous health. Such diseases as
befell the race were removed with ease by scientific
applications of that agency — life-giving as life-
destroying—which is inherent in vril. Even this
idea is not unknown above ground, though it has
generally been confined to enthusiasts or charlatans,
and emanates from confused notions about mesmerism, odic force, &c. Passing by such trivial

contrivances as wings, which every schoolboy knows
has been tried and found wanting, from the mythical
or pre-historical period, I proceed to that very
delicate question, urged of late as essential to the
perfect happiness of our human species by the two
most disturbing and potential influences on upper-
ground society,—Womankind and Philosophy.   I
mean, the Rights of Women.

"Now, it is allowed by Jurisprudists that it is
idle to talk of rights where there are not corresponding powers to enforce them; and above ground, for
some reason or other, man, in his physical force, in
the use of weapons offensive and defensive, when it
comes to positive personal contest, can, as a rule of
general application, master women. But among this
people there can be no doubt about the rights of
women, because, as I have before said, the Gy,
physically speaking, is bigger and stronger than the
An; and her will being also more resolute than his,
and will being essential to the direction of the vril
force, she can bring to bear upon him, more potent-
ly than he on herself, the mystical agency which
art can extract from the occult properties of nature.

Therefore all that our female philosophers above ground contend for as to rights of women, is conceded as a matter of course in this happy commonwealth. Besides such physical powers, the Gy-ei have (at least in youth) a keen desire for accomplishments and learning which exceeds that of the male; and thus they are the scholars, the professors —the learned portion, in short, of the community.

Of course, in this state of society the female establishes, as I have shown, her most valued privilege, that of choosing and courting her wedding partner. Without that privilege she would despise all the others. Now, above ground, we should not unreasonably apprehend that a female, thus potent and thus privileged, when she had fairly hunted us down and married us, would be very imperious and tyrannical. Not so with the Gy-ei: once married, the wings once suspended, and more amiable, complacent, docile mates, more sympathetic, more sinking their loftier capacities into the study of their husbands' comparatively frivolous tastes and whims, no poet could conceive in his visions of conjugal bliss. Lastly, among the more important charac-

teristics of the Vril-ya, as distinguished from our
mankind—lastly, and most important on the bear-
ings of their life and the peace of their commonwealths, is their universal agreement in the existence
of a merciful beneficent Deity, and of a future world
to the duration of which a century or two are moments too brief to waste upon thoughts of fame
and power and avarice; while with that agreement
is combined another—viz., since they can know
nothing as to the nature of that Deity beyond the
fact of His supreme goodness, nor of that future
world beyond the fact of its felicitous existence, so
their reason forbids all angry disputes on insoluble
questions. Thus they secure for that state in the
bowels of the earth what no community ever secured
under the light of the stars—all the blessings and
consolations of a religion without any of the evils
and calamities which are engendered by strife between one religion and another.

It would be, then, utterly impossible to deny
that the state of existence among the Vril-ya is
thus, as a whole, immeasurably more felicitous than
that of super-terrestrial races, and, realising the

dreams of our most sanguine philanthropists, almost
approaches to a poet's conception of some angeli-
cal order.   And yet, if you would take a thousand
of the best and most philosophical of human beings
you could find in London, Paris, Berlin, New York, or
even Boston, and place them as citizens in this beatified community, my belief is, that in less than a year
they would either die of *ennui*, or attempt some
revolution by which they would militate against the
good of the community, and be burnt into cinders
at the request of the Tur.

Certainly I have no desire to insinuate, through
the medium of this narrative, any ignorant dis-
paragement of the race to which I belong.   I have,
on the contrary, endeavoured to make it clear that
the principles which regulate the social system of
the Vril-ya forbid them to produce those individual
examples of human greatness which adorn the annals of the upper world.   Where there are no wars
there can be no Hannibal, no Washington, no Jack-
son, no Sheridan;—where states are so happy that
they fear no danger and desire no change, they
cannot give birth to a Demosthenes, a Webster, a

Sumner, a Wendel Holmes, or a Butler; and where
a society attains to a moral standard, in which there
are no crimes and no sorrows from which tragedy
can extract its aliment of pity and sorrow, no salient
vices or follies on which comedy can lavish its
mirthful satire, it has lost the chance of producing
a Shakespeare, or a Molière, or a Mrs. Beecher
Stowe. But if I have no desire to disparage my
fellow-men above ground in showing how much the
motives that impel the energies and ambition of individuals in a society of contest and struggle—become dormant or annulled in a society which aims
at securing for the aggregate the calm and innocent
felicity which we presume to be the lot of beatified
immortals; neither, on the other hand, have I the
wish to represent the commonwealths of the Vril-ya
as an ideal form of political society, to the attainment of which our own efforts of reform should be
directed. On the contrary, it is because we have
so combined, throughout the series of ages, the elements which compose human character, that it
would be utterly impossible for us to adopt the
modes of life, or to reconcile our passions to the

modes of thought, among the Vril-ya,—that I arrived
at the conviction that this people—though originally
not only of our human race, but, as seems to me
clear by the roots of their language, descended
from the same ancestors as the great Aryan family,
from which in varied streams has flowed the dominant civilisation of the world; and having, according
to their myths and their history, passed through
phases of society familiar to ourselves,—had yet
now developed into a distinct species with which it
was impossible that any community in the upper
world could amalgamate: And that ·if they ever
emerged from these nether recesses into the light of
day, they would, according to their own traditional
persuasions of their ultimate destiny, destroy and
replace our existent varieties of man.

It may, indeed, be said, since more than one
Gy could be found to conceive a partiality for so
ordinary a type of our super-terrestrial race as myself, that even if the Vril-ya did appear above
ground, we might be saved from extermination by
intermixture of race. But this is too sanguine a belief. Instances of such *misalliance* would be as rare

as those of intermarriage between the Anglo-Saxon emigrants and the Red Indians. Nor would time be allowed for the operation of familiar intercourse. The Vril-ya, on emerging, induced by the charm of a sunlit heaven to form their settlements above ground, would commence at once the work of destruction, seize upon the territories already cultivated, and clear off, without scruple, all the inhabitants who resisted that invasion. And considering their contempt for the institutions of Koom-Posh or Popular Government, and the pugnacious valour of my beloved countrymen, I believe that if the Vril-ya first appeared in free America—as, being the choicest portion of the habitable earth, they would doubtless be induced to do—and said, "This quarter of the globe we take; Citizens of a Koom-Posh, make way for the development of species in the Vril-ya," my brave compatriots would show fight, and not a soul of them would be left in this life, to rally round the Stars and Stripes, at the end of a week.

I now saw but little of Zee, save at meals, when the family assembled, and she was then reserved and silent. My apprehensions of danger from an

affection I had so little encouraged or deserved,
therefore, now faded away, but my dejection continued to increase. I pined for escape to the upper
world, but I racked my brains in vain for any
means to effect it. I was never permitted to wander
forth alone, so that I could not even visit the spot
on which I had alighted, and see if it were possible
to re-ascend to the mine. Nor even in the Silent
Hours, when the household was locked in sleep,
could I have let myself down from the lofty floor
in which my apartment was placed. I knew not
how to command the automata who stood mock-
ingly at my beck beside the wall, nor could I ascertain the springs by which were set in movement
the platforms that supplied the place of stairs. The
knowledge how to avail myself of these contrivances
had been purposely withheld from me. Oh, that I
could but have learned the use of wings, so freely
here at the service of every infant, then I might
have escaped from the casement, regained the rocks,
and buoyed myself aloft through the chasm of
which the perpendicular sides forbade place for
human footing!

CHAPTER XXVII.

ONE day, as I sat alone and brooding in my chamber, Taë flew in at the open window and alighted on the couch beside me. I was always pleased with the visits of a child, in whose society, if humbled, I was less eclipsed than in that of Ana who had completed their education and matured their understanding. And as I was permitted to wander forth with him for my companion, and as I longed to revisit the spot in which I had descended into the nether world, I hastened to ask him if he were at leisure for a stroll beyond the streets of the city. His countenance seemed to me graver than usual as he replied, "I came hither on purpose to invite you forth."

We soon found ourselves in the street, and had not got far from the house when we encountered five or six young Gy-ei, who were returning from the fields with baskets full of flowers, and chant-

ing a song in chorus as they walked. A young Gy
sings more often than she talks. They stopped on
seeing us, accosting Taë with familiar kindness,
and me with the courteous gallantry which dis-
tinguishes the Gy-ei in their manner towards our
weaker sex.

And here I may observe that, though a virgin
Gy is so frank in her courtship to the individual
she favours, there is nothing that approaches to
that general breadth and loudness of manner which
those young ladies of the Anglo-Saxon race, to
whom the distinguished epithet of 'fast' is accorded,
exhibit towards young gentlemen whom they do not
profess to love. No: the bearing of the Gy-ei
towards males in ordinary is very much that of
high-bred men in the gallant societies of the upper
world towards ladies whom they respect but do not
woo; deferential, complimentary, exquisitely polished
—what we should call 'chivalrous.'

Certainly I was a little put out by the number
of civil things addressed to my *amour propre*, which
were said to me by these courteous young Gy-ei.
In the world I came from, a man would have

thought himself aggrieved, treated with irony,
'chaffed' (if so vulgar a slang word may be allowed
on the authority of the popular novelists who use
it so freely), when one fair Gy complimented me
on the freshness of my complexion, another on the
choice of colours in my dress, a third, with a sly
smile, on the conquests I had made at Aph-Lin's
entertainment. But I knew already that all such
language was what the French call *banal*, and did
but express in the female mouth, below earth, that
sort of desire to pass for amiable with the opposite
sex which, above earth, arbitrary custom and hereditary transmission demonstrate by the mouth of
the male. And just as a high-bred young lady,
above earth, habituated to such compliments, feels
that she cannot, without impropriety, return them,
nor evince any great satisfaction at receiving them;
so I, who had learned polite manners at the house
of so wealthy and dignified a Minister of that
nation, could but smile and try to look pretty in
bashfully disclaiming the compliments showered
upon me. While we were thus talking, Taë's sister,
it seems, had seen us from the upper rooms of the

Royal Palace at the entrance of the town, and,
precipitating herself on her wings, alighted in the
midst of the group.

Singling me out, she said, though still with the
inimitable deference of manner which I have called
'chivalrous,' yet not without a certain abruptness
of tone which, as addressed to the weaker sex, Sir
Philip Sidney might have termed 'rustic,' "Why do
you never come to see us?"

While I was deliberating on the right answer to
give to this unlooked-for question, Tae said quickly
and sternly, "Sister, you forget—the stranger is of
my sex. It is not for persons of my sex, having
due regard for reputation and modesty, to lower
themselves by running after the society of yours."

This speech was received with evident approval
by the young Gy-ei in general; but Tae's sister
looked greatly abashed. Poor thing!—and a
PRINCESS too!

Just at this moment a shadow fell on the space
between me and the group; and, turning round, I
beheld the chief magistrate coming close upon us,
with the silent and stately pace peculiar to the Vril-

ya. At the sight of his countenance, the same terror which had seized me when I first beheld it returned. On that brow, in those eyes, there was that same indefinable something which marked the being of a race fatal to our own—that strange expression of serene exemption from our common cares and passions, of conscious superior power, compassionate and inflexible as that of a judge who pronounces doom. I shivered, and, inclining low, pressed the arm of my child-friend, and drew him onward silently. The Tur placed himself before our path, regarded me for a moment without speaking, then turned his eye quietly on his daughter's face, and, with a grave salutation to her and the other Gy-ei, went through the midst of the group, —still without a word.

CHAPTER XXVIIL

When Taë and I found ourselves alone on the broad road that lay between the city and the chasm through which I had descended into this region beneath the light of the stars and sun, I said under my breath, "Child and friend, there is a look in your father's face which appals me. I feel as if, in its awful tranquillity, I gazed upon death."

Taë did not immediately reply. He seemed agitated, and as if debating with himself by what words to soften some unwelcome intelligence. At last he said, "None of the Vril-ya fear death: do you?"

"The dread of death is implanted in the breasts of the race to which I belong. We can conquer it at the call of duty, of honour, of love. We can die for a truth, for a native land, for those who are dearer to us than ourselves. But if death do really threaten me now and here, where are such counteractions to the natural instinct which invests with awe and terror the contemplation of severance between soul and body?"

Taë looked surprised, but there was great tenderness in his voice as he replied, "I will tell my father what you say. I will entreat him to spare your life."

"He has, then, already decreed to destroy it?"

"'Tis my sister's fault or folly," said Taë, with some petulance. "But she spoke this morning to my father; and, after she had spoken, he summoned me, as a chief among the children who are commissioned to destroy such lives as threaten the community, and he said to me, 'Take thy vril staff, and seek the stranger who has made himself dear to thee. Be his end painless and prompt.'"

"And," I faltered, recoiling from the child—"and it is, then, for my murder that thus treacherously thou hast invited me forth? No, I cannot believe it. I cannot think thee guilty of such a crime."

"It is no crime to slay those who threaten the

good of the community; it would be a crime to slay the smallest insect that cannot harm us."

"If you mean that I threaten the good of the community because your sister honours me with the sort of preference which a child may feel for a strange plaything, it is not necessary to kill me. Let me return to the people I have left, and by the chasm through which I descended. With a slight help from you, I might do so now. You, by the aid of your wings, could fasten to the rocky ledge within the chasm the cord that you found, and have no doubt preserved. Do but that; assist me but to the spot from which I alighted, and I vanish from your world for ever, and as surely as if I were among the dead."

"The chasm through which you descended! Look round; we stand now on the very place where it yawned. What see you! Only solid rock. The chasm was closed, by the orders of Aph·Lin, as soon as communication between him and yourself was established in your trance, and he learned from your own lips the nature of the world from which you came. Do you not remember when Zee bade

me not question you as to yourself or your race!
On quitting you that day, Aph-Lin accosted me,
and said, 'No path between the stranger's home and
ours should be left unclosed, or the sorrow and evil
of his home may descend to ours. Take with thee
the children of thy band, smite the sides of the
cavern with your vril staves till the fall of their
fragments fills up every chink through which a
gleam of our lamps could force its way.'"

As the child spoke, I stared aghast at the blind
rocks before me. Huge and irregular, the granite
masses, showing by charred discoloration where they
had been shattered, rose from footing to roof-top;
not a cranny!

"All hope, then, is gone," I murmured, sinking
down on the craggy wayside, "and I shall never-
more see the sun." I covered my face with my
hands, and prayed to Him whose presence I had so
often forgotten when the heavens had declared His
handiwork. I felt His presence in the depths of
the nether earth, and amid the world of the grave.
I looked up, taking comfort and courage from my
prayers, and gazing with a quiet smile into the face

of the child, said, "Now, if thou must slay me, strike."

Tae shook his head gently. "Nay," he said, "my father's request is not so formally made as to leave me no choice. I will speak with him, and I may prevail to save thee. Strange that thou shouldst have that fear of death which we thought was only the instinct of the inferior creatures, to whom the conviction of another life has not been vouchsafed. With us, not an infant knows such a fear. Tell me, my dear Tish," he continued, after a little pause, "would it reconcile thee more to departure from this form of life to that form which lies on the other side of the moment called 'death,' did I share thy journey? If so, I will ask my father whether it be allowable for me to go with thee. I am one of our generation destined to emigrate, when of age for it, to some regions unknown within this world. I would just as soon emigrate now to regions un-known, in another world. The All-Good is no less there than here. Where is He not?"

"Child," said I, seeing by Tae's countenance that he spoke in serious earnest, "it is crime in thee to slay me; it were a crime not less in me to say, 'Slay thyself.' The All-Good chooses His own time to give us life, and His own time to take it away. Let us go back. If, on speaking with thy father, he decides on my death, give me the longest warning in thy power, so that I may pass the interval in self-preparation."

We walked back to the city, conversing but by fits and starts. We could not understand each other's reasonings, and I felt for the fair child, with his soft voice and beautiful face, much as a convict feels for the executioner who walks beside him to the place of doom.

CHAPTER XXIX.

In the midst of those hours set apart for sleep and constituting the night of the Vril-ya, I was awakened from the disturbed slumber into which I had not long fallen, by a hand on my shoulder. I started, and beheld Zee standing beside me.

"Hush," she said, in a whisper; "let no one hear us. Dost thou think that I have ceased to watch over thy safety because I could not win thy love? I have seen Taë. He has not prevailed with his father, who had meanwhile conferred with the three sages whom, in doubtful matters, he takes into council, and by their advice he has ordained thee to perish when the world re-awakens to life. I will save thee. Rise and dress."

Zee pointed to a table by the couch on which I saw the clothes I had worn on quitting the upper world, and which I had exchanged subsequently for the more picturesque garments of the Vril-ya.

The young Gy then moved towards the casement and stepped into the balcony, while hastily and wonderingly I donned my own habiliments. When I joined her on the balcony, her face was pale and rigid. Taking me by the hand, she said softly, "See how brightly the art of the Vril-ya has lighted up the world in which they dwell. To-morrow that world will be dark to me." She drew me back into the room without waiting for my answer, thence into the corridor, from which we descended into the hall. We passed into the deserted streets and along the broad upward road which wound beneath the rocks. Here, where there is neither day nor night, the Silent Hours are unutterably solemn,— the vast space illumined by mortal skill is so wholly without the sight and stir of mortal life. Soft as were our footsteps, their sounds vexed the ear, as out of harmony with the universal repose. I was aware in my own mind, though Zee said it not, that she had decided to assist my return to the upper world, and that we were bound towards the place from which I had descended. Her silence infected me, and commanded mine. And now we

19°

approached the chasm. It had been re-opened; not presenting, indeed, the same aspect as when I had emerged from it, but, through that closed wall of rock before which I had last stood with Taë, a new cleft had been riven, and along its blackened sides still glimmered sparks and smouldered embers. My upward gaze could not, however, penetrate more than a few feet into the darkness of the hollow void, and I stood dismayed, and wondering how that grim ascent was to be made.

Zee divined my doubt. "Fear not," said she, with a faint smile; "your return is assured. I began this work when the Silent Hours commenced, and all else were asleep: believe that I did not pause till the path back into thy world was clear. I shall be with thee a little while yet. We do not part until thou sayest, 'Go, for I need thee no more.'"

My heart smote me with remorse at these words. "Ah!" I exclaimed, "would that thou wert of my race or I of thine, then I should never say, 'I need thee no more.'"

"I bless thee for those words, and I shall remember them when thou art gone," answered the Gy, tenderly.

During this brief interchange of words, Zee had turned away from me, her form bent and her head bowed over her breast. Now, she rose to the full height of her grand stature, and stood fronting me. While she had been thus averted from my gaze, she had lighted up the circlet that she wore round her brow, so that it blazed as if it were a crown of stars. Not only her face and her form, but the atmosphere around, were illumined by the effulgence of the diadem.

"Now," said she, "put thine arms around me for the first and last time. Nay, thus; courage, and cling firm."

As she spoke her form dilated, the vast wings expanded. Clinging to her, I was borne aloft through the terrible chasm. The starry light from her forehead shot around and before us through the darkness. Brightly, and steadfastly, and swiftly as an angel may soar heavenward with the soul it rescues from the grave, went the flight of the Gy, till I heard in the distance the hum of human voices, the sounds of human toil. We halted on

the flooring of one of the galleries of the mine, and
beyond, in the vista, burned the dim, rare, feeble
lamps of the miners. Then I released my hold.
The Gy kissed me on my forehead passionately,
but as with a mother's passion, and said, as the
tears gushed from her eyes, "Farewell for ever.
Thou wilt not let me go into thy world—thou canst
never return to mine. Ere our household shake off
slumber, the rocks will have again closed over the
chasm, not to be re-opened by me, nor perhaps by
others, for ages yet unguessed. Think of me sometimes, and with kindness. When I reach the life
that lies beyond this speck in time, I shall look
round for thee. Even there, the world consigned
to thyself and thy people may have rocks and gulfs
which divide it from that in which I rejoin those of
my race that have gone before, and I may be
powerless to cleave way to regain thee as I have
cloven way to lose."

Her voice ceased. I heard the swan-like sough
of her wings, and saw the rays of her starry
diadem receding far and farther through the
gloom.

I sate myself down for some time, musing sorrowfully; then I rose and took my way with slow footsteps towards the place in which I heard the sounds of men. The miners I encountered were strange to me, of another nation than my own. They turned to look at me with some surprise, but finding that I could not answer their brief questions in their own language, they returned to their work and suffered me to pass on unmolested. In fine, I regained the mouth of the mine, little troubled by other interrogatories;—save those of a friendly official to whom I was known, and luckily he was too busy to talk much with me. I took care not to return to my former lodging, but hastened that very day to quit a neighbourhood where I could not long have escaped inquiries to which I could have given no satisfactory answers. I regained in safety my own country, in which I have been long peacefully settled, and engaged in practical business, till I retired, on a competent fortune, three years ago. I have been little invited and little tempted to talk of the rovings and adventures of my youth. Somewhat disappointed, as most men are, in matters connected with household love and domestic life, I often think of the young Gy as

I sit alone at night, and wonder how I could have rejected such a love, no matter what dangers attended it, or by what conditions it was restricted. Only, the more I think of a people calmly developing, in regions excluded from our sight and deemed uninhabitable by our sages, powers surpassing our most disciplined modes of force, and virtues to which our life, social and political, becomes antagonistic in proportion as our civilisation advances,—the more devoutly I pray that ages may yet elapse before there emerge into sunlight our inevitable destroyers. Being, however, frankly told by my physician that I am afflicted by a complaint which, though it gives little pain and no perceptible notice of its encroachments, may at any moment be fatal, I have thought it my duty to my fellow-men to place on record these forewarnings of The Coming Race.

THE END.

www.ingramcontent.com/pod-product-compliance
Lightning Source LLC
Chambersburg PA
CBHW020847020726
47497CB00005B/1289